T

By the same author:

Private Schulz (with Jack Pulman)
Bullshot
Bloodbath at the House of Death
Automan
Cover-Up
One Magic Christmas
Ruthless People

TIN MEN

A Novel by Martin Noble
Based on the Motion Picture from
Touchstone Pictures
Produced by Mark Johnson
Written and Directed by Barry Levinson

A STAR BOOK
published by
the Paperback Division of
W.H. ALLEN & Co. PLC

A Star Book
Published in 1987
by the Paperback Division of
W.H. Allen & Co. PLC
44 Hill Street, London W1X 8LB

Printed and bound in Great Britain by
Anchor Brendon Ltd, Tiptree, Essex

ISBN 0 352 32081 8

Prologue

Years later, in the smoky pool halls and shabby back offices of Baltimore, the tin men – those who'd survived the dark days of the Commission and had not handed in their licenses – would shudder and grimace when some keen young fresh-faced entrant into the world of aluminum siding would ask, after lapping up the tales of legendary scams that the veterans could rap off like tickertape, 'What really happened in 1963?'

It was a bad year. The worst. The year of the Commission.

The young hopefuls would look puzzled – then they'd turn wise with recognition. 'Oh, yeah, the *Commission!* Wasn't that all about some cover-up. "There'll be no whitewash at the White House"?'

'No, that was Watergate, it came ten years after.'

'Yeah? . . . 1963 . . . ? Hey, that was the year Kennedy got shot. That Warren Commission was some charade. Wasn't Ruby a Soviet agent? That's why he put Oswald out of the game—'

'No, I'm talking about the Home Improvements Commission.'

'Huh?'

And then the old tin men would talk about the Year that the Scamming Had to Stop . . . when brash young Ivy-Leaguers used the Commission as a stepping stone for their own political ambitions. Some good tin men got wiped out that year and it was never quite the same.

Sure, the scams started up again – dropping the five-dollar bill, the Life Magazine dodge, the showcase incentives – but once the fear got into your bones it got to be just another job. Once upon a time, the old guys would say, it was almost like Hollywood – you weren't just selling tin, but hopes and dreams; making folk feel their homes were as special as they were – and everybody won. The young guys, already working out their commission with a small 'c' and a big '$' on their calculators, would nod politely, recognising the bullshit: tin men with tin brains that had gotten so rusty they wouldn't even find their way down that yellow brick road – they were talking as much crap as the Wizard of Oz himself. Didn't that movie come out in '63, same year as the Beatles?

To be honest the old tin men would have had to admit to a certain amount of poetic license. It was easy to blame all the evil that had befallen the world since 1963 – the Bomb, the Recession, drugs, famine – on the Home Improvements Commission, but there had been other factors even way back then, a quarter of a century ago, that had destabilised the tin game.

Like the human factor.

And if a young hopeful should point this out, you could be sure an old retired salesman like Moe Gable would chuckle, order himself another scotch and say casually, 'Did I ever mention a coupla tin men by the name of BB and Tilley . . . ?'

Chapter One

As Bill Babowski stepped jauntily into the Cadillac showroom he mentally moved into top gear, pulling down the cuffs of his crisp white shirt, adjusting his tie and blazer. *Alert, alive, awake, aware, ATTITUDE!* he reminded himself. *You're the hottest-shot tin man in Baltimore . . . nobody can outdance you, and certainly not some jumped-up, two-bit car salesman!*

It was true that Babowski, or BB as he was known by one and all at the Superior Aluminum Siding Company, danced a mean Marengay – he was famous for it throughout the Baltimore tin community. Still a bachelor in his mid-thirties, BB had the manic energy and dapper elegance of a frisky tomcat.

Aware of the salesman's eyes on him, he circled the baby blue Cadillac cautiously, the doubt on his face concealing intense excitement. He'd had his eyes on this little beauty for several months and, thanks to a couple of delicious scams, he was now in a position to take possession of her. He'd treat her more lovingly than any wife or mistress. Here was one lady who'd not be messing up his life and, what's more, would keep her shape. This little baby blue wouldn't run to fat and would remain faithful to him. Nobody, but nobody, would get their bumpers on her bumper. With an unconscious gesture he tenderly stroked her bonnet . . .

'She's a beauty,' a solicitous voice came from behind him, as if in consent.

Caught off-guard, BB swung round and scrutinised the salesman suspiciously. He looked like a jerk and the cheap Italian box-jacket didn't help.

'Who?' BB snapped, pulling out a cigarette and, at the same time, dropping his lighter.

Automatically the salesman stooped to pick it up. 'What?' he said in bewilderment, handing back the lighter.

BB smiled to himself. 'Who's the beauty?' he said, returning the Lucky to the packet and replacing it with the lighter in his inside pocket.

The salesman looked even more confused. 'The car,' he replied uneasily.

BB feigned surprise. 'I thought maybe you saw some chick walking by. I lost my concentration.' He stared indifferently at the Cadillac. 'Why do they call cars "she"? They never say "he" . . . always "she".'

The salesman shrugged as BB walked one more time around the Cadillac. 'Very nice . . .' he muttered grudgingly. He couldn't wait to get her out on the road. 'Very nice.'

'You're a sick man!' Nora Tilley screamed up the stairs. 'Sick! Do ya hear me? *Do ya hear me*?'

What's the point? she thought miserably. He never heard her any more. He hadn't listened for years – maybe not since high school. Ernie had been so different then – so bright and funny, and full of ideas about what they would do with their lives. In the early years of their marriage, after he'd returned from Korea, he'd gone into salesmanship like a sinner embracing the Church.

Somewhere along the line Tilley had lost out on the action and been left behind. She wouldn't mind so much if, just for once, he'd admit he wasn't the hotshot he made himself out to be when he was out drinking with the tin men. She was now thirty-three, still attractive if she made the effort, but nowadays she was so worn out and washed-out who was to know? Not Tilley, for sure. He wouldn't even take her out into the country – which was what this row had been about, though it might as well have been about the weather. Nothing seemed to get through to him these days.

'Who's sick?' Tilley called down, peeking around the bannister as he came out of the upstairs bathroom. A year older than Nora he was still boyishly handsome – in spite of his short, stocky build and receding hairline.

'Who do ya think I'm screaming at?' she yelled up at him in exasperation. 'How many of you are there up there? There's only you, and you're a sick human being.'

As usual Tilley ignored her. 'Where's my white on white shirt?' he yawned, coming down a few steps. 'The nice one, you know.'

Nora closed her eyes and clenched her fists with frustration. 'It's like yelling through a wall to you,' she sighed. 'I'm carrying on about what a disgusting human being you are, and all you want to know is where your white on white shirt is.'

'Yes,' he replied evenly, 'the one with the permanent stays.'

Nora stared at him for a moment, then turned on her heel and retreated into the kitchen.

Chapter Two

The moment of truth had arrived.

'Now don't try to hustle me here... you know what I mean,' BB warned the salesman as they sat in the Cadillac dealership office going over the contract. 'I hate being hustled. Give me an honest price, not one of your "special" deals... give me an honest price. Do I make myself clear?'

Maybe he did, maybe he didn't. The salesman was in any case right out of his depth and was going by the book.

'Now, how much are you willing to pay?' he said nervously.

BB pulled a disgusted face. 'There ya go,' he snorted. 'There ya go... you're doing it... you're doing one of those hustle numbers.'

The salesman scratched his head. 'I'm just trying to get an idea how much you're willing to pay.'

'Four dollars...' BB leapt in firmly if not completely seriously. 'I want to pay four dollars a month.'

The salesman shook his head uneasily. 'That's not an honest answer.'

BB sighed. 'What do ya want to hear? That I'd love to pay three hundred and fifty a month... is that what you want to hear? Tell me how much you want me to pay and I'll tell you how much I'll pay, but don't do a hustle on me... I don't like that. How much do I want to pay? I'd like to pay nothing!'

That could be arranged, the salesman was about to

reply, but stopped himself just in time, though he still found himself nodding, unable to conceal his admiration.

'You're . . .' he cleared his throat, 'you're in the business yourself?'

BB smiled with satisfaction.

Tilley had enough trouble making sense of what was going on around him these days – the old scams just didn't seem to work like they used to, he couldn't remember the last time he'd made a decent sale and he was up to his neck in debt to the company – and that wasn't counting the unpaid bills and IOUs he was accumulating. And now Nora was giving him a hard time.

'You're being unreasonable,' she shouted after him as he left the house, his tie undone around his white on white shirt, and clutching his sports jacket. 'You don't even want to listen.'

Tilley shook his head. 'I don't know what I did . . .' he said innocently. 'I got no idea. If it's my fault, I'm sorry . . . I can do no better than that. A full unconditional apology.' He walked down the steps to his Cadillac – bought in a golden age when he could have every mark from Baltimore to Washington signing up for tin by the square mile with just a little sweet talk and the shake of a fountain pen. Magic moments . . . By now he should have a fleet of Cadillacs and his own business but it just hadn't worked out like he'd figured it should.

As Tilley got into his Cadillac and started the engine, his wife stood watching on the porch, a solitary figure in a neighbourhood of hundreds of duplicate houses.

Down at the Cadillac dealership the salesman was feeling a measure of relief: at least he'd made the sale, though this guy sure drove one hell of a hard bargain. He felt like he'd been put through a mincing machine.

'If you even have the smallest problem,' he said unctuously, 'call me personally and I'll just shoot you straight into the service department.' BB still maintained an air of deep suspicion. 'And I get a loaner if the car's got to stay?'

'As we discussed, you get a car if the car has to be kept overnight.'

'I get a loaner?' BB repeated.

The salesman nodded.

At last BB took out his pen, giving the salesman one final searching look . . . and signed.

There was an audible sigh of relief from both parties.

'She's gonna drive me to my grave,' Tilley mumbled to himself as he drove bleary-eyed past the Washington Monument. 'I'm headed to my grave . . . it's not supposed to happen this way.'

He winced and moved his head around, stretching his neck in a slow, painful circular action. 'It's not even eleven o'clock and my neck is stiffening up.'

He jutted out his jaw. 'My neck's tight . . . it's tight.'

He noticed a red light ahead and began to slow down, but continued to roll his head this way and that.

At the very same moment, a shiny baby blue Cadillac, with BB at the wheel, was reversing out of the car lot. BB spotted the red light in his front driving mirror but continued backing out into the street.

Rolling back his head, Tilley slowed down to fifteen miles an hour and BB seeing the rusty dark blue Cadillac in his mirror continued to back into the street, assuming the other car would stop—

It didn't.

Seconds later, the two Cadillacs crashed into each other and every atom of the entire right rear of BB's brand new shiny baby blue Cadillac was instantly and forever rearranged. For maybe half a minute the two men sat in their respective Cadillacs, shocked and confused. Then, as though orchestrated by some demonic conductor they bolted from their cars to examine the damage, and as Tilley gazed with horror at his buckled hood, BB raced up and the two men stood eyeball to eyeball glaring at each other.

'Are you a lunatic?' BB bawled. 'Can't you see I'm trying to back out of this lot? There's a red light, you shoulda stopped.'

'Me?' Tilley yelled back indignantly. 'What are you, crazy? You just want to back into the middle of the street like that. A man's just driving along and you back into the middle of the street. What kind of driving is that? What kind of driving?'

'There's a red light,' BB stormed, 'I'm making a space for myself... that's what I'm doing, in order to get into the street... that's something ya do!'

Tilley looked around for witnesses. 'You came out of nowhere... you bolted out of no place...' He still couldn't believe this. 'Bolted out of nowhere...'

'Bolted!' BB exploded back. 'At six miles an hour I'm bolting into the street!' Why did he have to live on the same planet with a lunatic like this little jerk? 'You schmuck!' he screamed. 'You schmuck!'

He began to move towards Tilley menacingly.

'Back away from me, do ya hear me?' Tilley threatened unconvincingly. 'Back away from me.'

'Back away?' BB snarled. 'You want me to back away? I'll back away.'

He turned ostentatiously to walk away from Tilley and then whisked round and kicked in the headlights of the rusty dark blue Cadillac.

Tilley stared in horror at his beloved car and then back at BB.

'You're a fucking lunatic!' he yelled, and in a blind

rage he threw himself at BB, locking his hands around BB's neck and trying to throttle him. The two men fell on to the trunk of BB's car and tried to squeeze the life out of each other as a crowd began to gather around them. The bravest jumped in and tried to pull the two tin men apart.

'You're a mad man!' BB gasped, appealing to the public for support. 'Smashes into me, attacks me . . . the man is crazy!'

'Come on, no,' said a big black guy who was trying to get a hold on BB's arm. 'Calm down, calm down.'

Another man had his arms round Tilley and was fruitlessly attempting to prise him away. 'Take it easy,' he spluttered. 'Take it easy.'

'Get this guy!' Tilley shouted to the crowd. 'Will ya get this guy? Backs in front of me, and then kicks my headlight in . . . And *I'm* crazy. You lunatic!'

He made another jump for BB and again several bystanders moved forward to pull them apart.

'You're going to prison,' BB gasped. 'Death! Death! They're going to give you death!'

When at last the two were separated, BB turned to gaze incredulously at his brand new Cadillac with the smashed-in side.

'Car only has one sixteenth of a mile, and I've been hit,' he muttered, as though he'd been personally fractured.

He swung back to Tilley who was examining his smashed-in headlight.

'I'm gonna get even with you, you son of a bitch,' BB snarled. 'I'm gonna get even with you. This is no ordinary traffic accident.'

Tilley's eyes narrowed. 'You want to drive a Cadillac,' he hissed back, 'learn how to drive. You want to get even with somebody? You picked the wrong person to get even with. Nobody backs into traffic, smashes my car and says they want to get even.' His eyes narrowed even further until they were practically invisible. '*I'm* gonna get even!'

Chapter Three

'Did ya see *Bonanza* last night?' growled Sam Pickles, a heavyset man in his fifties, shaking his head sadly as he delicately buttered his toast. The three tin men were seated in a diner booth having their late morning breakfast. A mood of good-natured lethargy had descended on them.

The other two shook their heads indifferently.

'Can you tell me,' Sam went on, ignoring this, 'why Ben Cartwright had a colored guy stay over?'

Gil Glickstein, halfway through pouring a pound of sugar into his coffee, looked up with mild curiosity.

'Ben Cartwright had a colored guy stay overnight at the Ponderosa?' He gave the third salesman an almost imperceptible wink. It was something to lighten up the morning a little.

Mouse, who was picking his teeth with a matchbook, cast an investigative squint at Sam.

'Did he know this guy personally?' Mouse said casually.

Sam pondered a moment. 'No,' he remembered. 'He was just passing through, asked if he could stay over, and Ben Cartwright said, "Sure thing."' He took a bite of toast and frowned. 'It doesn't make any sense... he invites him in to stay. Is that crazy or what? If a colored guy came to my door and said, "Can I stay the night?" I'd tell him, "Get the fuck out of here!"' He darted a quick look at Gil and Mouse. 'It's nothing personal, mind you.'

Mouse nodded understandingly and winked at Gil. 'You're not a bigot, is that what you're telling us?'

Sam looked astonished at the suggestion. 'Me?' he said indignantly. 'No, I'm not a bigot.'

'If you're not, how come you're making such a big thing out of it?' said Gil.

Sam threw him a look as if to say, I thought that would be obvious. 'It's the fact that Ben Cartwright's on the Ponderosa . . . he's in the middle of nowhere. It's not like he's living on Reistertown Road with houses all round . . . we're talking about the West here. It's the idea that a strange guy comes to the door in the middle of the West.' It hadn't been like that before the war – or even five, ten years ago – before all this civil rights shenanigan. 'It doesn't make sense,' he muttered, 'that's all I'm saying.'

'Come on . . .' Mouse smirked, 'you're a bigot, that's what you are.'

'Listen,' said Sam indignantly, 'I'll sell tin to anybody . . . I don't care who he is. A mark's a mark, whether he's Chinese, Indian or from Mars . . . I'm thoroughly integrated. Makes no difference to me . . . I just wouldn't have one of those guys sleep in my house.'

The morning was looking brighter every minute for Gil and Mouse.

Still fuming, Tilley parked his battered Cadillac and walked into the diner, making for the booth where the other tin men of the Gibraltar Aluminum Siding Company were seated.

'Florence,' he shouted out to the depressed-looking waitress, 'eggs and the toast, the way I like it.'

'Not too gooey,' she replied dispiritedly. 'Coffee right away.'

'... I just don't believe that *Bonanza* is an accurate depiction of the West,' Sam was concluding the case for the prosecution. 'I say no more.'

'Come on,' Tilley grumbled, as he slipped into the booth next to Sam, 'give me a couple of more inches.'

Sam held up his toast in mock surrender. 'You want me to take my plate ... I'll eat in the parking lot.'

Tilley sighed. 'Come on, Sam, give me a break. I'm having a terrible morning. You're not going to believe this, some guy just crashed into me ... right in the middle of the street ... then he attacks me.' He was still shaking at the memory. 'One of the loonies.'

Sam looked heartbroken as he munched his toast. 'Did ya live?' he said nonchalantly.

'Did you get his name?' Mouse asked.

'Yeah, I got his name,' Tilley said darkly. 'The police came ...' He banged his fist on the table. 'God, I can't believe it ... the guy's an idiot.'

He pulled a piece of paper from the pocket of his sports jacket and peered at it. 'Yeah, here it is ... he's got some Polish name ... Babowski ... Bill Babowski ... fucking son of a bitch.'

'I know the guy,' Gil chipped in excitedly. 'They call him BB.'

Tilley stared at Gil as though he were an accessory to the crime – or at least guilty by association. 'You know the son of a bitch.'

'Yeah,' Gil grinned. 'He works with Bagel.'

Tilley was seized with a sudden attack of nausea. 'He sells aluminum siding? I don't believe it ...' He cupped a hand over his brow. 'Of all the people that could run into me, it has to be a fucking tin man. How come I don't know him?'

Gil shrugged. 'You musta seen him. He hangs out with Carly Benelli, Cheese ... you know, that group.'

Tilley shook his head firmly. 'I don't know the guy,'

he said with distaste.

'Don't you remember,' Gil insisted, 'he was up at the Corral one night when we were there... he's a good dancer. You must have seen him.'

'I don't know the guy,' Tilley stuck to his guns, as though he were a subpoenaed witness at a McCarthy trial.

'Gil,' Sam said helpfully, 'he doesn't know the guy.'

Gil looked completely foxed. 'I thought he knew him, Sam... I can't believe he doesn't know him.'

'He seems to be indicating that he doesn't know him,' Sam said confidentially, like he was Tilley's attorney.

'I don't know the guy!' Tilley exploded.

'He's a good dancer,' Gil reminded him.

Tilley rounded on him. 'What do you want me to do, date him?' he bawled. 'What do I give a shit if he's a good dancer?'

'I thought you saw him,' Gil went on remorselessly. 'I was amazed, he does a Marengay—' he held out his hands to indicate just what inadequate tools mere words were to describe the brilliance of BB's Marengay. 'I tell you, if I was a girl I'd be impressed.'

'You're *not* a girl and you're impressed,' Sam pointed out drily.

The arrival of Florence with Tilley's coffee adjourned the case.

'Is it fresh?' Tilley asked dubiously.

'Yes, it's fresh,' she yawned and slammed it down on the table.

'Just asking, Florence,' Tilley muttered.

'You're always just asking,' she grumbled as she walked back to the bar.

'I'm telling you, you just can't believe how well this guy does the Marengay,' Gil sighed, seemingly obsessed with this Gene Kelly of the tin world.

Tilley growled and gritted his teeth. 'I'll tell you one

thing: when I get a hold of this guy, I'll break both his legs and then he won't dance the Marengay too good.'

Chapter Four

The Superior Aluminum Siding Company office occupied part of the second floor of a run-down building in an industrial park dominated by steelworks, a few miles inland from Chesapeake Bay. A row of half a dozen Cadillacs – none of them brand new but, equally, none of them as smashed-up as the baby blue Cadillac that had just parked alongside them – indicated that business was, if not booming, humming along nicely.

The office itself was filled with second-hand furniture in a conglomeration of styles, mostly mismatched. In one corner of the room two or three girls were working the telephones, canvassing interest in a demonstration of the unique benefits of aluminum siding. They had all clearly been trained to speak in the same hypnotically congenial tone of voice.

'Good morning,' one was saying blandly, 'I represent the Superior Aluminum Siding Company. We will have a representative in your neighborhood today. Would you be interested in seeing the benefits of our aluminum product.' She cupped a hand over the receiver and yawned. 'Yes . . . well, we do aluminum siding which improves the appearance of your house, and improves the insulation . . .'

At the next phone another girl was repeating the litany.

'. . . which improves the appearance of your house, and improves the insulation . . .'

'... Superior Aluminum Siding Company,' repeated a third girl. 'We will have a representative in your neighborhood today...'

In another corner of the room four tin men were sitting around a desk playing cards.

'So the guy goes to the doctor for a physical...' Moe Gable was saying. It was a joke he must have told thousands of times but Moe, now in his early fifties, had a way of telling you stories like they'd just happened the other day – which was maybe why his track record as a tin salesman was second to none. But this morning he was having a hard time, and that was because of Cheese who had this way of deliberately not getting the point. Cheese was one hell of a salesman because he had a skin as thick as aluminum but he was a bastard to play cards with or tell jokes to.

'... They do all those tests,' Moe went on, 'all that stuff, blah, blah, blah...

'... Doctor says, "When we get all the information back, we'll give you a call." Leaves the doctor. One day the telephone rings... the guy goes and picks it up.'

Cheese frowned. 'The guy?'

'The *guy*!' Moe repeated, immediately aggravated.

'Not the doctor?' said Cheese innocently.

Moe glanced at him quickly. 'That's right, the *guy* picks it up. He gets a phone call... it's the doctor on the line. Doctor says, "I've got some bad news and some worse news."'

BB, still in a silent rage, had walked into the office, fixed himself a coffee, and now came over to listen to the end of the joke.

'Guy says, "Well, let me hear the bad news first."

'"The bad news is, you've got twenty-four hours to live."

'The guy says, "What's the worse news?"

'Doctor says, "I forgot to call you yesterday."'

They all laughed, except BB.

'It's good . . . I like it,' said Looney, a thin guy who tended to twitch and blink a lot.

'I never heard bad news and worse news,' Cheese had to admit, '. . . smart joke.'

'Yeah . . . I like it,' Looney repeated, grinning broadly.

'It's dumb, but good,' Carly Benelli agreed.

BB, standing behind Cheese, stared morosely through his colleagues as they carried on with the card game.

'Up it fifty cents,' Cheese muttered.

'I call . . . I call,' said Looney. 'I'm in on this one . . . I call.'

'We get it,' Moe nodded, 'you're calling.'

Carly was clearly in two minds whether to stay in the game. 'I'm not sure,' he said nervously.

Irresistibly, BB found himself being drawn into the game.

'Stay with him,' he muttered to Carly.

'I don't know,' Carly agonised, biting his lip.

'Carly, get out of the hand . . .' Cheese said threateningly. 'I'm holding serious cards. *Very* serious cards.'

'He's bluffing,' BB advised.

Cheese chuckled. 'If I'm lying, I'm dying.' Carly's nerve instantly broke.

'I'm out,' he muttered, throwing in his hand.

'Ballsy move,' BB remarked sardonically.

'Did you get the new Cadillac?' said Moe, also throwing in his hand and turning to BB.

The older tin man was proud of his protégé: he'd taught Babowski everything he knew and had seen him develop from a young, arrogant, know-nothing who had failed to make it as an actor, had a chip on his shoulder a mile wide and used to mouth up some half-digested crap he'd gotten out of those half-assed intellectuals like Kerouac or Sallinger who all the young kids were reading back in the Fifties – into a confident, dynamic, though, let's face it, still arrogant tin man.

BB could have sold tin to his own grandmother in her grave. He could even sell it to other tin men – and had been known to do so when some brash young over-confident newcomer to the tin game needed putting in his place. But beneath all the wise-guy routine Moe knew that BB was as straight as they came. Thing about him was, he was a careful man. If BB had bought a new Cadillac you could bet your ass he could sell it three years later as brand new, and in a way there'd be no lie.

BB was still apparently studying the game with a fixed, almost wooden expression, and Moe was forced to repeat the question.

'Yeah,' BB muttered. 'It's already been hit.'

'What?'

A vein throbbed near BB's temple so Moe knew he was mad as hell.

'Didn't have it five minutes, backing out of the place, and a guy comes out of nowhere and bangs into my car.'

Looney was on tenterhooks – not to hear about the damage to BB's car but the damage to his own wallet.

'So, what ya got?'

'Pair of sixes,' Cheese replied breezily, throwing his hand down.

Looney couldn't contain himself. He let out a whoop of joy and showed his hand. 'Jacks. Win.'

Carly couldn't believe this. He'd had three queens.

'Shit!' he muttered. 'Pair of sixes!'

Moe ignored them. 'How much damage?' he asked.

'I bet it's six hundred bucks,' BB replied, looking a little ill.

Looney whistled. 'Six hundred bucks? I'd get rid of the car. That much damage it won't be any good. You may have dented the frame.'

'I didn't dent the frame,' BB said quietly.

Looney blinked. 'When you hit the frame, the car

doesn't ride right.'

BB's self-control snapped.

'He didn't hit the frame!' he stormed, and then pulled himself together. 'I'll tell you this,' he carried on in a measured, steely tone, 'I'm gonna get the son of a bitch. If he would have apologised or something, but this guy gets out, tries to push me around.'

'You're kidding me?' said Cheese, surprise mixed with muted irony.

'Yeah . . .' BB muttered. 'The guy's totally off the wall.'

He took a sip of his coffee and added thickly, 'I'm gonna get him . . . just for the fun of it.'

Chapter Five

Most days the tin men followed up leads the telephone canvassers had landed, usually allowing two or three hours to sweet-talk the mark though sometimes it could take much longer. The ones who were really hungry were sometimes known to stay up half the night, not leaving until the mark had signed on the dotted line. Then it was a contest of stamina and will, most often with a husband trying to impress his wife that he could screw the salesman for the best deal.

By that time the hapless wife – who'd first succumbed to a cold call and who had earlier in the evening formed an alliance with the salesman to persuade her tired spouse (who only wanted to eat his dinner, have a beer and catch the late show) not to throw the intruder out onto the street – had herself become just another pawn in a contest of male egos, and had gone to bed wishing she'd never let the salesman in her house in the first place.

The challenge of a cold call could sometimes be used to remotivate and inspire a tin man who was finding the job too easy: when boredom set in the gap between success and failure could narrow to the size of a yawn. As Moe well knew, they could also be useful to help the concentration of a salesman whose mind was on other matters. Like BB's was.

So it was no accident that they arrived early in the residential area where they were due to follow up a lead. It was a lower middle-class neighborhood of shabby houses that looked to be about thirty or forty years old.

'Now, let me see ...' Moe muttered, looking through his papers, 'we gotta be at the Hickey house at four.' He looked at his watch. 'It's about three-twenty now ... we've got some time on our hands. You want to get some coffee?'

BB, who was driving his battered new Cadillac, pulled a face. 'No, I'm up to here with the coffee.'

'They got any good pool halls around here?' Moe said innocently. It wasn't that kind of neighborhood.

'I don't know,' BB said abstractedly. Then his eyes lit up. 'You know what would be fun to do? ... Let's try the Life Magazine routine.'

Moe smiled.

'Yeah.'

Sometimes BB was still like putty in his hands.

'You know, I think we've got to come over about two feet,' BB said as he peered through the lens of a 35mm camera.

He moved the tripod on which the camera was mounted towards the window of the wooden-framed house they had been viewing. Through the curtains Mrs Doris Lacey watched suspiciously as the two men approached with their equipment.

'I think this is a better position ...' BB was saying loudly. 'The light is hitting it, which is accentuating the effect we're going for. It's very good ... very good.'

Moe struck a creative pose and practically called out. 'This shows the flaws in the creative structure ...'

'Yeah,' Moe whispered back, and looked businesslike.

'This is going to be terrific in Life Magazine,' BB went on in a loud, clear voice. *'Terrific in Life Magazine!'* he repeated as though shouting through a director's megaphone, then muttered wheedlingly, 'Come on outside, honey.'

'This should be our single biggest issue of Life Magazine,' Moe shouted.

A moment later the front door opened and Doris Lacey appeared on the porch.

'Bingo!' BB crowed quietly.

She was a thin, harrassed looking housewife and she approached them with suspicion and curiosity.

'Excuse me,' she demanded in a slightly whining voice. 'What are you doing?'

Moe stepped forward briskly. 'Oh, I hope we're not disturbing you, Ma'am,' he said solicitously. 'We're with Life Magazine . . . we'll be out of here in just a minute.'

BB appeared to be concentrating on his craft.

'Move the tripod another foot . . .' he said to Moe as he peered through the camera, 'another foot.'

'What do you mean, Life Magazine?' said Mrs Lacey, intrigued, as Moe moved the tripod.

At last BB looked up from the camera.

'Two minutes, Ma'am, and we'll be out of here. We just need the picture for Life Magazine, and we'll be out of here.'

Mrs Lacey was falling like a ripe peach. 'Life Magazine?' she repeated, maybe hoping her neighbors were listening. 'I don't understand.'

'It's very simple,' BB explained. 'Ya know, we're doing this layout about the benefits of aluminum siding – a "before" and "after" kind of presentation.'

The bullet had struck.

'A "before" picture?' she said with a touch of dismay.

Moe began to move in for the kill.

'So they see your house,' he said brightly, 'and another one done with aluminum siding . . . the other house looking so much more beautiful.'

'In Life Magazine?' she repeated faintly.

'It's a special issue on home improvements,' Moe went on, 'and ways to beautify your home.'

'A wonderful issue . . .' BB leaped in, 'it's one of the finest pictorial things we've done here at Life' – he repeated the word like a priest invoking the Holy Spirit – '. . . the ways you can improve your house.' He adjusted the camera as if about to do a major shoot. 'We're gonna be out of here in no time, Ma'am.'

Moe looked serious. 'It's gonna look very good, BB.'

At last Mrs Lacey came up with the correct line.

'My house is going to be the "before",' she said anxiously. 'Can't mine be like the "after"?'

BB appeared to consider this for a moment and then dismiss the idea. 'No, no . . .' he said apologetically, 'we've got a house that looked like yours and it's been done in aluminum . . . it's very nice.'

'Yeah,' Moe added with relish, 'really shows the *contrast* of what a house can look like.'

Mrs Lacey was looking thoughtful. 'What does it cost?' she asked, trying to sound casual.

'What? The aluminum siding?' said BB innocently. 'Oh . . . I don't know the figures off hand. Do you have any idea, Moe?'

'I think it's fairly reasonable,' Moe replied as though he'd never given it much thought.

There was a new note of desperation creeping into Mrs Lacey's voice as she asked, 'Could my house be the "after" in Life Magazine and you get another house for the "before"?'

BB frowned as though such an idea had never before impinged on his consciousness.

'Let me get this straight,' he said slowly. 'You mean, have your house as the "after" and find another house for the 'before"?'

Mrs Lacey's eyes had widened with excitement. 'Is it possible?' she said breathlessly.

BB hesitated. 'What do you think, Moe?' he said doubtfully. 'Would that be ethical?'

Moe scratched his grey hair. 'Well, we didn't sign any agreement with the "after" house,' he deliberated. 'All the same, we'd have to move very quickly, Ma'am... you know what I mean?'

BB seemed to be trying to figure this out. 'You'd have to work out an arrangement with an aluminum siding company and they'd have to do the job very quickly for us to make our deadline... we've got a deadline, that's our problem.'

'How quickly?' she asked anxiously.

Moe and BB exchanged glances.

'BB, what do you think?' Moe said. 'Can we slide the deadline, or what? Six or seven days?'

BB looked even more doubtful. 'Pressing it. Do you think we could manage it, Moe?'

'It's pushing it, BB.' Moe turned back to Mrs Lacey. 'What time would your husband be home, 'cos he'd have to go over the figures with the salesman... that's if there's a salesman available this evening.'

'He'll be home at seven,' she replied almost beseechingly.

'We might be able to work it,' said BB, the smashed-in Cadillac now forgotten.

Mrs Lacey oozed gratitude. 'That would be wonderful,' she sighed.

Four hours later, having signed up the Hickeys, BB and Moe were back at the Laceys, sitting on the Sears and Roebuck sofa sipping coffee, and looking almost like members of the family.

Mr and Mrs Lacey meanwhile were sitting across the dining room table from Carly who was quickly going through the specification, adding up the figures.

'Okay,' he finally announced, 'we've got a total of thirty-seven hundred dollars.'

'Thirty-seven hundred dollars?' said the hapless

husband, turning green.

'Jack, honey, we're gonna be in Life Magazine,' Doris reminded him. BB glanced at Moe, it was time to turn the heat up a little. 'Moe,' he said quickly, 'did you call the office and make sure we can hold up the issue until this job is completed? This house really could be a showcase.'

Jack Lacey was still mesmerised by the bottom line. 'Thirty-seven hundred dollars!' he repeated in horrified disbelief.

Carly came to the rescue. 'I tell you what,' he said, like he was prepared to make an exception just this once, like he was feeling particularly well-disposed towards these people because they were good, decent folk, like he was going out on a limb here and it might maybe cost him his job but so what. 'I've got an idea. Do you mind my guys working on a Saturday? 'Cos if my crew can work on Saturday next, that'll free my guys up on Monday.'

Jack Lacey was hanging on, waiting for the payoff.

'Yeah,' Carly went on unhurriedly, 'that'll really help me out on another job. Anyway, if we can do that, I think I'll be able to knock off three hundred and fifty dollars from the job. You see, I've got an overlapping situation on Monday . . . I don't want to go into it. What do ya think?' he ended, looking from one Lacey to the other. 'We got a deal?'

Jack didn't even blink. 'Yep,' he said instantly.

Chapter Six

'You make me feel so young,' Sinatra sang. 'You make me feel like spring has sprung...'

Sam Pickles sat contentedly in the passenger seat of Tilley's Cadillac, puffing away on his cigar and tapping his brown suede shoe along to the Nelson Riddle beat as he sang along with unmelodious gusto, the cigar sticking firmly in his mouth giving Sinatra an unfair advantage in the duet.

Inside the house, Tilley was having a hard time.

'No, I'm sorry, Mr Tilley,' a tough-looking construction worker said impassively as the tin man packed up his sample case, 'I just can't afford it.'

Tilley looked desperately at the man's wife who sat quietly by her husband's side on a couch across from him.

'We haven't even got to discussing terms,' he made a last-ditch effort. 'There are so many friendly financial arrangements that would hardly be a bite into your weekly salary.'

The man had clearly lost interest the moment Tilley had told him the cost. 'No... not this time,' he said, pointedly looking at his watch.

'Well, as I said,' Tilley began to dither, 'you can always reach me... you've got my card, and when the time comes, let's talk.'

The couple stood up and showed him to the door.

'Hey,' he suddenly remembered, 'give my best to your

little son . . . wonderful kid there. What's his name again, Ronnie?'

'Randy,' said the husband curtly.

'Randy,' Tilley corrected himself, 'right. Well, goodnight.'

Sam was accepting Frank's invitation to come fly away with him when Tilley stormed out of the house and threw the sample case into the back of the car.

'I thought I had 'em . . .' he snarled angrily, climbing into the driver's seat and slamming the door. 'I was this close.' He held up a finger and thumb.

Sam nodded sympathetically and stubbed out his cigar. 'The amount of time you spent there, I thought you were ready to send for me to close it up.'

'Damn!' Tilly muttered. 'I thought I had 'em.'

He started up the car wondering if somebody up there had it in for him.

The bar at the Pimlico hotel was an ideal place to conduct business with his staff as far as Wing was concerned. The warmth and intimacy of the bar restaurant put everyone at ease so that the guys who'd not made a sale and missed out on their commission wouldn't feel so bad. There was no sense in increasing low morale.

John Wing – head of the Gibraltar Aluminum Siding Company – was a tall, strong, imposing figure, a natural leader cursed with an easy-going nature. A pilot in World War II, he was reputed to have been shot down somewhere in the Sahara and entered civilian life with a Purple Heart, a hole as big as a lemon in his right shoulder and the promise of a great career behind a desk in the USAF, but for reasons best known to himself he decided he was not the company type. And so he'd moved in on the tin game where a salesman was as good as his last pitch and he could be a big fish in a small, informal and roughly democratic pond . . . And where he could cut a few corners, break a few rules and, maybe, make a lot of bucks. Even so, Wing had been having a few sleepless nights lately with all the rumors of a Commission that could put them all out of business.

Around the table sat Mouse, Sam, Tilley, Gil and several other tin men as Wing held court, reviewing a stack of estimates, contracts and sales ledgers as if his office desk had been transported to the bar. He was looking through the specifications, sales agreement and financial report on a sale Mouse had just concluded and nodded approvingly.

'Forty-six hundred dollars,' he said with satisfaction. 'This looks like a sound deal. They own their own house . . . We won't have any problems getting the financing for them. Real good, Mouse.'

Mouse grinned as Wing picked up his check book ledger and wrote out a check.

'So that's one thousand, one hundred and thirty-eight dollars,' Wing muttered and handed the check to Mouse.

'Thanks boss,' Mouse beamed, pocketing the check. 'Pleasure doing business with ya.'

Wing turned to Tilley and Sam. 'Now what's your story, you guys?'

Tilley cleared his throat. 'Nothing again . . .' he admitted in embarrassment, 'came up short. Let me get a little advance . . . three hundred, just to carry me for a bit.'

Wing sighed. 'Tilley, I'm already carrying you for, what is it – twenty-three hundred? Something like that?'

Tilley waved his hand dismissively. 'No problem – just in a little slump here.'

Wing threw him a suspicious glance. 'Don't try to go walking on me.'

'What do you mean, walking?' Tilley protested indignantly. 'You think I'm gonna work somewhere else, you're wrong . . . you've been very good to me . . . very honorable.'

Sam rushed to Tilley's defence. 'He's always said that about you, Wing. Always said that about you . . . he has.'

Wing hesitated. 'I'll give you hundred and fifty,' he said reluctantly.

One thing Tilley hated was begging. He had his pride but he also had his back against the wall and what was a guy to do?

'Wing, I need a bit more than that . . . I got expenses,' he mumbled.

'What's wrong with your wife?' Wing said sternly. 'She doesn't work?'

In Wing's experience when a guy fell down on his sales you could blame it on his domestic situation. He knew Nora and Tilley hadn't been seeing eye to eye lately but he couldn't keep financing their marriage. Business, after all, was business.

'Yeah, she works,' Tilley replied morosely, 'but how much is she gonna make working at the Social Security Office?'

Wing wrote out the check and handed it to him.

'Come on, Wing,' Tilley wheedled, 'can't you do better than this . . . a man in my position in terms of this firm . . . I dunno . . .'

Wing sighed again. Was he going soft? 'All right, I'll give you two hundred.'

He corrected the check and handed it to Tilley.

'Honey,' Mouse yelled over to a cocktail waitress, 'can you get me some Marlboros and a 7 and 7?'

'And some Scotch, straight up,' Sam added.

Tilley slipped the check in his pocket feeling like a charity case. If he could just work out a few new scams it could make all the difference to his life – with Nora, with his place in the company, and with his own sagging morale. He felt like he was sinking into a pit and all he needed was a foothold to get out of it. How come a schmuck like Mouse could make five grand for the firm while he, Tilley, hadn't even earnt a dime? Yes, even just one original scam would do it. Like if he could get the mark to think he was getting the tin for free...

'Now listen, guys,' Wing was saying gruffly. 'We got a problem here.'

'Did she hear me say Scotch straight up?' Sam asked Mouse.

Wing looked and sounded serious, and soon got the tin men's attention. 'My sources tell me this Home Improvement Commission is for real... It's no jackpot. These guys are going to be a real pain in the ass, so any of the scams that you guys are pulling, they get wind of it, they take your license and it's goodbye to this business.'

The tin men stared at him disbelievingly.

'They take away your license?' Mouse echoed in horror. 'They take away your livelihood? What kind of people are these?'

'They have no respect for the working man,' Sam muttered.

'Which scams are they talking about?' said Tilley. 'They got a list?'

Unless these guys were mind-readers they couldn't take away your license for a scam they didn't have on the books. Anyway how did they decide what was a scam and what was just smart selling?

Wing more or less spelt it out. 'Any irregularities, you know, selling a house on the pretense that it's a model house and every job sold in the area they get a kickback... the Life Magazine hustle...' He shrugged. 'You guys know all the bullshit numbers we can run.'

'Jesus! What a pain in the ass,' Sam summed it up for all of them. 'Do you think this Commission's gonna stick around or is it gone with the wind?'

Tilley was having trouble taking this in. It was one

more kick in the gut.

'They take your license?' he repeated softly.

It had been a good night's work for Moe and BB and as they drove back into the city they were already spinning fantasies of what they'd do with their first million.

'I wouldn't mind seeing Africa some time,' Moe remarked.

BB pulled a face. 'Not me. I don't want to go where they've got snakes.'

Moe raised an eyebrow. 'They've got snakes?'

BB loved all this. 'I've heard they've got snakes that'll outrun a horse through the grass,' he moved into the spiel. 'They got a snake that bites you . . . you got eleven seconds to live. I'll tell ya something I once heard from this guy I used to know who went out to Africa. He . . . Hold it!'

Violently he slammed down the brakes.

'What's wrong?' Moe said in alarm.

BB was already backing his Cadillac half way up the street. He brought it to a halt in the driveway of the Pimlico Hotel parking lot.

'This guy who ran into me,' he said thickly. 'That's his car.'

He drove the car into the park and opened the car door. 'I'll be back, Moe,' he said tersely. 'I'm gonna even the score.'

Quickly he walked over to the rusty dark blue Cadillac which he'd backed into – or, as he saw it, had driven into him – and with a swift kick, smashed in the one headlight that wasn't already broken.

'Give me eight points I take the Knicks over the Lakers for twenty,' Tilley said to Mouse as they were putting their coats on to leave the Pimlico.

Mouse shook his head. 'It's too big a spread.'

From the other side of the hotel door there was the sound of breaking glass. Tilley turned to peer through the glass doors and then his face went white with anger.

Outside in the car park the hotshot Marengay man was kicking in the headlight of Tilley's car.

'It's that fucking lunatic again,' he screamed as BB ran off towards his own car.

Followed by several of the tin men, Tilley raced out of the hotel door towards BB's Cadillac which instantly pulled away and speeded off down the street.

'Can you believe this guy,' he stormed as he stood on the sidewalk watching BB's car disappear. 'Is he sane or what?'

'Isn't that something,' Mouse commiserated.

'What's he got, a gnat up his ass?' said Sam. 'What the hell's wrong with the guy?'

Gil was getting excited again. 'Don't you recognise him from the Corral?'

In Tilley's present state nothing could have been calculated to infuriate him more.

'I don't know the guy!' he seethed.

Gil whistled with admiration. 'I'll never forget his Marengay.'

Tilley slammed a clenched fist into his cupped hand. 'I'll tell you something, if Mr Marengay wants to play . . . we'll play.'

Chapter Seven

By the time Tilley arrived home, well past midnight, he felt like a zombie. Wearily he let himself into the house and went through to the kitchen where Nora was sitting, drinking a cup of coffee and working on a three-week-old crossword puzzle.

She didn't bother to look up as he took off his coat and threw it on a chair.

'Look at you,' she murmured, 'quarter to three and home already. What happened? You and the fellas run out of things to talk about?'

He closed his eyes. 'Please! I'm out there working myself to the bone, trying to make a living.'

He walked over to the refrigerator and poured himself an orange juice.

'What's a five-letter word for a Portuguese overseas province?'

'Try Macao,' he said absently.

'M – A – C – A – O . . . that fits.' She yawned.

Tilley gazed at his wife. 'What're you doing up so late?'

'I'm not working tomorrow.'

He looked around the kitchen. It was more like a playroom/study with bookcases full of Reader's Digests, cookery books, romantic fiction paperbacks and detective thrillers which Nora devoured – she subscribed to half a dozen book clubs and still managed to get through several library books a week; there was an old table with a sewing machine in one corner; a rocking chair they'd bought for her mother back in 1959 – a year before she passed away; she'd even installed her record player down here to listen to her stack of Jim Reeves and Brenda Lee 45s.

'I think this place may be a little too large for us,' he said casually.

Nora looked up for the first time and stared at him in surprise. 'What are you talking about . . . this matchbox?'

He began to pace the kitchen floor. 'It's got a lot of overhead to it. What do you do . . . you spend your time in the bedroom and the kitchen, that's all. So why do you need a living room and a dining room?'

He walked over to the back door and looked out. 'Why do ya need a backyard?'

Nora guessed the truth. 'You're not selling anything?'

He sighed. 'I'm in a slump.'

'It happens,' she said more gently.

He ran a plump hand through his thinning hair. 'Last year I'm number three top seller . . . year before, right up there. I can't get my momentum going this year.'

He sat down at the table and rubbed a stubby hand through his thinning hair.

'Well, you will,' Nora said sympathetically. 'You always do.'

'I'm not sure I like the idea of all this overhead breathing down my neck,' he resumed the attack. 'When you have a place like this, that's a lot of overhead.'

'What are you talking about?' she said sharply. 'The monthly payments on your Cadillac are more than this whole house. Why don't you get yourself something cheaper, like a Chevy?'

He waved his hand at the suggestion. 'It doesn't instil confidence in my clients. Cadillac means that you're dealing with someone of importance.' His spirits sagged. 'I thought I had a couple tonight . . . They just slipped away . . . slipped away.'

'I'm gonna take a bath,' he said, stretching and standing up. 'My neck's been tight since this morning.'

'I'll turn out the lights,' Nora sighed, getting up and putting the cups in the sink.

Tilley lay in the bathtub, dozing off as the hot lather relaxed him and eased the pain in his neck. Soon the memory of Mr Marengay, of the lost sale and of every other godawful thing that had happened to him that day receded as he succumbed to blissful sleep . . .

'Are you listening to me, Tilley?'

'Huh?'

'. . . I said, we hardly ever do things together.'

He stared up at her uncomprehending.

'Like what?'

Did she want to get in the bath with him or what?

'Do things together that are enjoyable.'

He didn't get it. 'What would we do together for it to be enjoyable?'

She hesitated. 'If we want on a picnic . . . it would be fun.'

There she went, on about the picnic again.

'I don't understand a picnic,' said Tilley. 'We just go some place . . . we put a thing on the ground, and we eat.'

'Yes . . . it's nice to do that.'

'Why? I don't get it,' he said, washing himself quickly. 'It's better sitting at home and watching TV.'

'I think there's something nice about a picnic . . .' Nora said quietly. 'It's fun.'

He shrugged. 'What's fun about it? Ants get into the food . . . there's bees. I don't get it. We have to drive, it takes maybe an hour to get there, then you sit in grass and eat. Why is that fun?'

Nora was close to tears. 'I just thought it might be nice to do something together, that's all . . . thought it might be fun.'

'It doesn't sound like fun to me,' he sniffed. 'You take the stuff you've got here in the house, you take it some place to eat it. It's just as much fun eating in front of the TV, and we do that together, don't we? No ants and no bees . . . much more comfortable.'

'It's not the same thing.'

'Scrub my back will ya, Nora,' he yawned.

Automatically she picked up the back brush, put soap on it and began scrubbing his back.

'Not too hard!' he grumbled.

She stopped, held her breath and then carried on more gently.

'Don't get me wrong,' Tilley said, 'I'm willing to do anything with you. I'm just a little stymied by a picnic. If you want to go, send me a postcard.'

With a little cry of frustration, Nora dropped the brush in the tub and rushed out of the bathroom. Tilley stared after her and then fished the back brush out of the water.

'What did I say?' he muttered.

Chapter Eight

'I think you make a left here,' said Gil as Tilley drove his Cadillac at a furious speed through the industrial park where Gibraltar's rival company was situated.

'Yeah . . . there it is . . .' Gil shouted excitedly. 'That's the place . . . Superior Aluminum that's who he works for . . . that's it over there.'

Tilley pulled the car to a screeching halt, and leaving the engine running, reached over to the backseat.

'Okay, Mr Marengay . . .' he muttered, 'here I come.'

'Hey, Tilley, don't go too wild,' said Gil, nervously watching as Tilley extracted a crowbar from his tool bag and got out of the car.

'I'll show the son of a bitch,' he muttered, as he ran across to BB's Cadillac and proceeded to smash in the windshield and all the windows of the car.

'He'll get a lot of air,' he grunted as he wielded the crowbar for one final onslaught. 'Won't be too stuffy in this car when I'm finished.'

'Quick, Tilley,' Gil called from Tilley's Cadillac, 'let's get out of here.'

Tilley didn't need to be told twice: he raced back to his car and drove off at full speed leaving BB's brand new baby blue Cadillac open to the inspection of Baltimore's birds and bees.

One more colored pin went into the map of a fifteen-block area of Baltimore marking out yet another

Superior Aluminum conquest.

'That was a good sale, Double B,' said Bagel. 'Just got a call on a loan . . . we're in business.'

Bagel was Wing's counterpart at Superior, though physically they couldn't have been more different. Where Wing was tall, lean, always smartly dressed, with a fondness for expensive suits and an almost Roman bearing, Bagel was a little guy who wore baggy pants held up with suspenders and had never been seen without his black fedora hat. And where, in a sense, Wing had worked his way down into the tin game, Bagel had started at the bottom and was fond of letting people know it.

'This whole section has been very fertile for us,' he was telling BB.

In another part of the office Moe, Looney and Carly were standing with a young guy in his early twenties, dressed in a fashionable Ivy League suit and nodded politely as the tin men vied with each other to impress him with their knowledge and experience.

'Sure you wanna get into the tin game?' said Moe.

'Money's good, I understand,' Stanley Franks remarked in a cultured Boston accent.

Looney twitched furiously. 'Lot of crazy people you're gonna run into when you're knocking on those doors,' he pointed out. 'Hermits that don't see the outside world, Jehovah's Witnesses that try and sell you the Bible at the same time you're trying to sell them tin. People that are just lonely and want to have conversations.'

Looney could never figure out why he seemed to get more than his fair share of weirdos – 'Birds of a feather' was Cheese's explanation.

'Every time you step in that door, you've got to be fast on your feet,' Carly cautioned the new recruit.

'Interesting,' said Stanley, and his interest was clearly

genuine.

'What's the best way to qualify a mark?' Moe quizzed him.

'What?'

Moe grinned. 'How do you know if you can get the upper hand? How do you know if you're dealing with a guy who's in an inferior position to you, or superior position? How do you know?'

This barrage of questions had the effect of putting Stanley on the defensive. 'You just have to talk and feel your way,' he said weakly.

Moe moved in. 'Quick way . . . get a book of matches out of your pockets to light your cigarette, okay? . . . then you drop the matches on the floor.'

'Yeah?' Stanley looked puzzled.

'Guy bends down to pick up the matches for you, you got a mark . . . you got this guy in your pocket. If he looks to you to pick it up, you've got a long hard, tough sell on your hands.'

'You want to get in good with these people?' said BB, walking over to join them, having poured himself a coffee. 'You want to win their confidence? Good thing to try . . .' To demonstrate, he opened his wallet. 'Get a five dollar bill, take it out when the guy's not looking, drop it on the ground. Guy looks back, pick it up, hand it to him and say, "Mr Blah Blah, you musta dropped this five dollar bill on the ground."

'Two things happen: he says, "It's not mine," you say, "Musta been, 'cos it's certainly not mine," or the guy takes it. Right away this guy is thinking you must be one hell of a nice guy . . . you're in. You start chipping away . . . you start getting inside those people.'

Stanley seemed to be almost mesmerised by all this information but BB suddenly looked at his watch, put down his cup and grabbed his coat.

'Come on, Moe,' he said hurriedly, 'let's split.'

'Yeah,' Looney said, giving Stanley a nudge, 'we'd better go. Come on, Stanley. Me and Stanley,' he quipped to Carly, 'it's like a first date.'

As BB and Moe walked out of the Superior Aluminum Siding building the first sight to greet them was the baby blue Cadillac, open to the world.

The blood drained from BB's face.

'What?' said Looney cheerfully as he caught up with them. 'You got a special bargain when you bought this car? They come cheaper without windows?'

BB surveyed the smashed in windows in grim silence, then reached into the car and picked up a handful of broken glass, tossing it up and down in his hands, his mind spinning.

'This guy's looking to play tit for tat,' he said in a strange, distorted voice. 'That's not my game. I'm gonna play hardball.'

He threw the glass down on the ground.

'What's going on?' Stanley asked Looney in a hushed voice.

At this point Looney had the tact to keep his mouth shut: he simply nodded for them to go and they walked over to Looney's Cadillac.

'I'm gonna find out everything about this son of a bitch,' BB was saying, 'and then I'm gonna find the one thing that cuts him to the quick.'

'Let's go inside,' Moe said quietly. 'Make some calls.'

BB was about to say something but instead he nodded and they started back inside.

Chapter Nine

The pool ball ricocheted off an eight ball which dropped with awful neatness into the pocket. Tilley threw down his pool stick in disgust.

'Damn it!' he muttered. 'Damn it! I can't believe it . . . I can't believe I did that.'

'Well then, believe it,' Mouse said smugly. 'There's no sense not to believe it, because you did it . . . so believe it. That's twenty more . . . you owe me sixty.'

'You think I can't add?' Tilley snapped.

Mouse put a nickel in the juke box and, as Harry Belafonte began to sing 'The Banana Boat Song', he joined in.

'"Dayo! . . . Da, da, da, da, day. Daylight come and he wanna go home . . ."'

The noise that came from somewhere inside Mouse was excruciating and only added to Tilley's irritation. But Mouse was by now completely caught up in the song.

'Oh, this is going to be good,' Gil quipped as Mouse crescendoed to the climax.

'"*Dayo! . . . Da, da, da, da, da, da, da, da, da, da, da, da, da-dayo—*"' He slammed his pool cue on the ground for emphasis. '"Daylight come and he wanna go home . . ."'

Wing ran his business from several locations. Apart from the bar restaurant of the Pimlico Hotel, he had a table at the Corral Club and even held informal conferences at the Pimlico Race Track. But Gibraltar's main offices were situated in the back of the pool hall and it was here that Sam Pickles was catching up on his paperwork when he came across an unopened letter from the IRS addressed to Mr Ernest Tilley. He examined the post date mark and noticed it was over five weeks old – dated 3 January 1963.

'Jesus Christ!' he muttered and hurried through to the pool hall where Mouse was still screeching along to 'The Banana Boat Song'.

Tilley had just finished racking the balls as Sam came through the door.

'Tilley,' said Sam, giving him a discreet nod, and as Tilley joined him he handed him the letter, adding quietly, 'Found this on your desk while I was going over some papers.'

Tilley glanced at it with mild curiosity and deep distaste.

'From the IRS,' he said uncomfortably. 'I never even remember seeing it. I must have left it with my other bills. I wonder what it is?'

'Maybe it's a refund check,' Sam said without much conviction as Tilley opened the envelope.

'Hum, says here that they haven't received my 1961 taxes, nor my check for four thousand dollars for 1960.' Tilley scowled and tucked the letter away in his pocket.

'What?' said Sam, concerned. 'It must be a clerical error.'

'I can't believe they spend all that time and energy to write to me . . . to single me out,' Tilley said angrily.

Sam stared at him. 'What are you talking about?'

He shrugged. 'I probably forgot . . . people forget their taxes all the time . . . just slipped my mind . . . I got so many things on my mind.'

They had reached the 'office' and Sam took a bottle of

Scotch out of his drawer and poured them both a glass.

'What about the four thousand dollars?' he said dubiously. 'It just slipped your mind to pay your taxes . . . four thousand dollars?'

Tilley drank his whiskey and sighed. 'I figured they could wait a few years . . . it's not like they need my money to build a bomber. You think they're waiting for my money before they dig a new road? Are they all sitting there saying, "Well, it's time we went to see that guy on Pimlico Road . . . can't run this government without his four thousand dollars".'

He sat back in his chair. 'I figured they'd give me a little leeway. I'm going to pay them . . . I know I've got a debt . . . I just a needed a little leeway.'

Sam shook his head wisely. 'You can't mess around with the government. Why don't you go to H & R block – they'll take care of your taxes for you.'

'You think I'm gonna let some schmuck know all my business?' Tilley growled angrily. 'Have some guy pull me over the coals for spending on this and that? I need some privacy.'

Some people would call Sam Pickles an old-fashioned guy but he still believed in Uncle Sam and the rule of law. No one liked paying their taxes but he'd been a young man during the Thirties' Depression and had seen the miracle Roosevelt had brought about with his New Deal. A guy like him, a tin man, did a job, it wasn't just a job: it was helping the national economy. Maybe one day he and Tilley would be out on the streets themselves if this Commission had its way and they'd both be grateful for any social security handout they could get. In any case, it didn't do to mess around with the IRS – these guys meant business.

'Taxes is serious stuff, Tilley,' he said gruffly.

Tilley didn't seem to hear him. He was too hung up on the idea that his privacy was being invaded by a schmuck who, oddly enough, had a strong resemblance to Mr Marengay.

'I can just see that schmuck in that little tax shop telling people my business,' he snarled. 'How much I make... how much I spend... no way!'

Sam was experienced enough as a salesman to know when a pitch wasn't working. It was time to talk tough. 'All I can say, is you better get a lawyer or somebody to look into this, 'cos the IRS, they don't fuck around.'

'Just what I need in my life right now,' Tilley muttered bitterly. 'I'm in a slump and I've got the IRS on me. Like when something goes wrong, it's like everything goes wrong at the same time, it's like...'

A picture rose up in his mind of Mr Marengay standing over him sneering, *You're going to prison. Death! They're going to give you death!...*

He took another shot of whiskey and wondered where all this was going to end. Maybe Nora was right: maybe what they both needed was to get away somewhere. Maybe a picnic wasn't such a bad idea after all. Suddenly he felt a rush of affection for her. Whatever happened, at least, she'd stick by him...

Chapter Ten

To celebrate her day off work from the Social Security Nora watched a couple of soaps on the TV and then planned what she was going to cook for dinner that evening. There was enough chicken left over to make a risotto but she was short on vegetables: maybe there was enough for herself. Even if Tilley did get back before midnight he wouldn't notice she'd cooked. If he had his way they'd live on TV dinners, except she refused to buy them. Even a slob like Tilley deserved better than that.

She knew he was in a slump and she'd tried to sympathise but what was the point? If he'd had a good year he'd only go and buy himself another Cadillac, that's what all the tin men did. It was a kind of status symbol with them. If only just for once he'd pay some attention to her. It wasn't asking much to take her out for a picnic and maybe he'd even enjoy it if he just made the effort.

If you want to go send me a postcard...

The bastard. He could damn well fix his own dinner. She watched the end of *Dr Kildare* and switched off the television. Perhaps she would go down to the supermarket; she could drop in on the library on her way back – maybe Harold Robbins' *Carpetbaggers* would be in. It was supposed to be quite sexy, but she'd also heard it was a great story and she needed something she could really get lost in. Come to think of it, she could do with some sex too, but not out of a book – the real thing. One thing was for sure: she wasn't going to get it from Tilley. He'd forgotten what the word meant.

She grabbed her coat and the car keys to her old Chevy which Tilley had bought her secondhand in a fit of generosity and left the house.

Outside, two men sat in a dark brown Cadillac and watched as she got into her car, started the engine and pulled away.

'That must be her,' muttered BB, sitting shotgun in Moe's car.

They followed her.

Ten seconds after Nora entered the local supermarket BB walked in, pulled a shopping cart from the stall and wandered up behind her, quickly extracting a pile of frozen dinners from the freezer.

Outside in the street Moe watched through the window as Nora stopped with her cart further down the frozen food section, deciding which vegetables to buy.

'Are these any good, do ya know?' said BB casually. 'These TV dinners?'

Nora swung round to see a smartly-dressed and quite attractive-looking man, maybe a few years younger than Tilley, with a pile of frozen dinners in his arms.

'I don't think they're too good for you,' she replied a little nervously, 'not a lot of 'em anyway.'

She turned back to the vegetables but BB had only just begun.

'My wife died,' he said hoarsely.

Nora looked at him again, this time with some sympathy. 'Oh, I'm sorry to hear that.'

BB bravely shrugged off her pity. 'I'm over it now,' he said manfully, 'but it was a very trying time for me . . . very trying . . . I've only just started eating again.'

Nora gazed at him and thought, here was a man who'd appreciate her cooking.

'You know what would be a lot more healthy and satisfying is to get yourself a chicken,' she said gently. 'Just pop it in the oven for a couple of hours with a little bit of seasoning on it. Makes a good meal, and you can make sandwiches with the leftovers.'

BB stared at her with surprise and intense gratitude. Then his face fell.

'But then,' he said in a choked voice. 'You have to sit and watch it cook. Something seems sad about a man sitting alone in a house and watching a chicken cook.'

She was almost tempted to ask him back home there and then. After all, who else would appreciate her cooking so much as this poor, sad, lonely . . . and now she came to look at him . . . really quite handsome widower? Next to him, Tilley was a sick, disgusting human being . . .

Out in the street, Moe watched as BB said something to Tilley's wife which made her laugh. Then she said something back to him and he laughed, taking hold of her arm.

'He's an amazing sort,' Moe said to himself, 'he's got the gift.'

Across the street from the supermarket a man in a business suit was sitting behind the wheel of a plain-looking Ford. A car pulled up behind him and Stanley Franks, Superior's new tin man, got out and walked over to the other driver. He knelt down and had a brief, intense conversation with him. Finally Stanley nodded and tapped the side of the car, which drove off. Then he walked back to his own car and sped away.

Chapter Eleven

'Thank you, Mr Tilley,' a mousie little man wearing a seersucker suit and bow tie said gratefully as he sat with his wife – his female equivalent – and swallowed it whole. Tilley had struck gold.

'I can't believe it,' said Horace Hudson, turning to his wife for confirmation that he had heard correctly. 'This is the most generous thing anyone's ever done . . . Swell! Like a gift from heaven.'

Tilley could hardly believe it himself. Maybe there was a God up there after all.

'The Lord has certainly blessed us this evening,' Mrs Horace Hudson agreed in a kind of muted ecstasy.

Tilley looked abashed. 'Well, what can I say.' He stood up to leave. 'I'm a modest person . . . I just do what I can to help.'

'Thanks again,' Horace Hudson said at the door, shaking his hand.

'So, what's the scoop?' Sam asked as Tilley climbed back into the passenger seat.

'We got 'em!' Tilley announced excitedly.

'You're kidding!' said Sam in amazement. For a start it was a cold call in the kind of neighborhood where they saved their last cent for the collection box in church. And Tilley's recent sales record had been about as successful as his luck at the races, in other words, zilch.

'Take a look at this, Sam,' Tilley said smugly.

Sam stared at the written contract for forty-two

hundred dollars worth of aluminum siding. Written across the top of the contract in Tilley's own big, bold, black handwriting were the words:

THIS JOB IS FREE

'Are you fucking crazy?' Sam exclaimed. 'You just gave them forty-two thousand dollars in aluminum siding free!'

Tilley bared his teeth in a wide, self-satisfied grin. 'This is the best scam I've ever thought of in my whole life.' He kissed his own hand ecstatically. 'It's in my blood... I'm brilliant... I'm fucking brilliant... this is such a brilliant scam I can't believe it... I'm beside myself.'

Sam stared at him in alarm. Maybe he was cracking up. 'What are you talking about?' he said nervously.

'Here it is... you go back in the house and this is what you say...'

'Mr Tilley is crazy,' Sam broke the news. 'He had a nervous breakdown.'

Mr and Mrs Hudson stared at him in astonishment.

'What's that?' said Horace uneasily.

'He's been under a lot of pressure recently... he snapped... he had a nervous breakdown.' Sam sighed. 'It's the saddest thing I've ever seen. Let's be honest about it, nobody gives away forty-two hundred dollars worth of aluminum siding free.'

Horace Hudson looked crestfallen. 'I thought it was very generous, but sometimes the Lord moves in mysterious ways.'

'Let me tell you something,' Sam said confidentially, 'when I go and see his boss and show him this contract... he'll lose his home... his wife and kids will be thrown out onto the street. He'll probably spend some time in an institution, so God knows what will happen to his wife and kids. Anyway,' he added briskly as though he'd said more than he should have, 'it's not your problem.'

He made as if to leave.

'Why do they have to be thrown out onto the street?' Horace asked on cue.

Sam turned back. 'You don't expect his boss to pick up the forty-two hundred job, do ya?'

'Hmm.' Horace glanced at his wife, torn between his Christian sense of charity and a feeling of merciful release.

'Yeah, it's a bad state of affairs,' Sam muttered, playing for time.

There was an uncomfortable pause.

'Let me ask you something, sir,' Sam said casually.

'Yes?'

'You don't think there's some way you could work with me to try and resolve this, do you?'

Hudson frowned. 'How so?'

Sam took a deep breath.

'Let's look at it this way, what if I can sell you this job at a wholesale price . . . kind of lessens the burden. The big boss won't get so angry, and maybe won't throw the guy's wife and kids out . . . at least they'll have a roof over their heads.'

Horace was hooked. 'What kind of wholesale price are we talking about?'

'You got a cup of coffee?' Sam said genially.

Mrs Hudson jumped to her feet. 'I'll get you a coffee . . . won't be a minute.'

'Let's just sit down and kick this around,' Sam grinned as Mrs Hudson disappeared into the kitchen.

Horace nodded and, as he turned to sit down, Sam quickly dropped a five dollar bill on the floor.

'What are you doing throwing your money around?'

Sam said bending down to pick it up.

'What's that?' said Horace curiously.

'I found a five dollar bill, here by the side of the chair,' Sam said, handing it over with an engaging smile.

Chapter Twelve

The Corral Club was crowded to the seams and jumping with activity. While a local band, Johnny and the Surfers, pounded out last year's hits on the tiny stage, BB was out on the floor dancing with a blonde girl he'd met that evening, and proving just why he'd acquired his reputation as a good mover.

The crowd loved it.

Meanwhile at the bar, Looney and Carly were filling Stanley in on some of the famous scams of the tin trade.

'The Buzzard had a great gimmick,' Carly was saying. 'You know, when it came time to measure a job, he'd cut the yardstick and re-glue it together . . . he took out seven inches so his square footage would always be higher. That way he's always make a few extra bucks on the job.'

'You're kidding,' Stanley laughed, lapping it all up.

'Yeah . . . he'd always put his hand over the break when he was measuring. Nobody looks at a yardstick to see how long it is.'

'I never did that,' Looney giggled, 'I never did that . . . I was never very good in arts and crafts. I could never make the ruler come out right.'

As the 'Locomotion' finished, BB gave his dancing partner a friendly pat on her rear: she walked back to her table and BB walked over to where Moe was sitting.

'Here's to Nora,' he said, toasting her in her absence with a beer can.

Moe grinned and they finished off their beers.

Back at the bar, Stanley was hungry for more.

'What else?' he prompted the tin men. 'Give me another story . . . these stories are great!'

'Just a minute . . .' Looney thought for a moment. 'I've got one. You know it's like the faster you can start spiking a job, the guy can't back out of the deal. Shoe had some customers that he thought was fragile on coming for the buy. He'd say to the guy, "Here, let me show you how bad a shape your house in in," and he'd rip off a piece of wood, maybe fifteen feet wide. The guy's house looks like shit so it makes it hard for him to back out of the deal when half the side of his house is missing.'

Looney shook his head with admiration. 'The Shoe's a fucking wonder.'

Tilley was still drunk with victory as they drove back through the city.

'Fantastic, Sam! A twenty-seven hundred sale! "This job is free!" What a beaut! I'm out of the slump! Tilley's riding high again . . . Tilley's back! We ought to go and celebrate. Let's go to the Corral and have a drink . . . we can turn the paperwork in a little later.'

'Gil says that's where "Marengay" hangs out,' Sam reminded him.

Tilley pulled a face. 'Gil keeps saying it . . . I've never seen him.' He laughed hysterically and hit the dashboard. 'I'm riding high . . . twenty-seven hundred dollars . . . "This job is free" . . . the man went insane . . . lost control of himself . . . his wife and children are out on the street!' He laughed even louder. 'Sometimes I'm brilliant . . . I'm fucking brilliant . . . I can't believe it.'

For a moment Sam wondered whether Tilley really was heading for a nervous breakdown.

BB was giving Moe a brief guided tour through the joys of bachelorhood.

'See that one,' he said pointing to a predatory-looking girl in her mid-twenties who was sitting at a table with her husband or boyfriend and running her fingers through his hair. 'If you were married to that one two weeks you'd have to put your head out of the window for air . . . this one smothers.'

He looked across to another girl, a strikingly pretty but moody looking brunette who was doing little to hide her anger at her boyfriend's interest in a flirtatious blonde.

'That one is the kind that can't live without you,' BB concluded, then added in a whining voice, '"Where were you? When will you be home?"'

Moe looked at his watch. 'I should get out of here,' he said a little anxiously. 'I told my wife I'd be home early tonight.'

'Christ! It's not even one o'clock yet.' BB eyed his friend pityingly. 'How long have you been married now? What is it? Twelve . . . twelve years?'

'Sixteen,' Moe admitted.

'Holy God! Sixteen years?' To BB it sounded like a life sentence. Longest he'd put up with a broad was six days. Dorian was a nice, obliging girl who'd made no demands on him – a guy needs his privacy – but six days with her was like sixteen years of married hell to BB. *Sixteen years!*

'What do you think?' he asked Moe. 'Is it worth it?'

Moe hesitated. 'Yeah,' he said with reasonable conviction.

'Why do you think?'

For once Moe was at a loss for words. 'It's hard to answer,' he replied, thinking of May and the kid, the good times and the bad times, like that Christmas back in '54 when she'd left him after a row . . . she was back a week later. He could still remember the look on her face when he'd opened the door and she was standing there with Leonard – he'd have been about six by that time –

and she looked kind of lost, like a young girl...

'Seems better than if she wasn't there,' he said simply.

'Quite a recommendation,' BB laughed sceptically. 'Can't wait to do it.'

As they carried on talking, the door to the bar opened behind them.

'Scotch straight up?' said Tilley.

'Yeah,' Sam replied.

'Scotch straight up and a rum and Coke for me,' Tilley said to the barman, then looked around at all the women who seemed to be crowding out the bar.

'Looks like there's good action here tonight,' he said with a hint of regret.

'What do you expect,' Sam grinned. 'It's half price night for divorced women. The place is hopping.'

BB was sounding forth on his theory of marriage 1963 style. 'Look how much more complicated things are now,' he said, surveying the Corral's clientèle with a jaundiced eye. 'There used to be a time you met a girl, you courted and then you got married and lived happily ever after. Now, see that one over there –' he pointed to a table where a heavily made-up blonde was drinking down Scotches faster than her boyfriend could order them '– that's Helen Armstrong... maiden name used to be Tudor. Get this: she dated Charlie Rider when I was in high school – seemed like they were together forever. They broke up; she started to go with Lenny Mardigian; they got married – she's Helen Mardigian. That goes on two years... three years, something like that. They divorce. Dates Billy Small for a couple of years; lives with John Isaacs for a year, marries Tommy Selnini... that marriage goes in the toilet, but fast. Now she's dating Charlie Rider who was divorced by Evelyn Chartoff who used to be Evelyn Gage before that.'

He shook his head and laughed wryly. 'So much for relationships.'

Chapter Thirteen

'I'm beginning to believe in God,' Sam announced as they sat at the bar.

Tilley eyed him suspiciously. 'You were never one of those atheists were you?'

'No, I'm not saying that, but I'm beginning to give God more thought.'

'So, what did you do?' said Tilley. 'Have some kind of religious experience?'

Sam looked serious. 'I tell ya . . . I took my wife for lunch yesterday . . . we went and had some smorgasbord, and it kind of happened.'

Tilley raised an eyebrow. 'You found God at the smorgasbord?'

'Yeah.'

'Sam, people have religious experiences like on a lake or when they go up into the mountains, that kind of thing.'

Sam was unimpressed. 'Maybe . . . but I had mine in a smorgasbord.'

'Sam, you're too much,' Tilley laughed.

'I went to get myself a salad and I started to see all these vegetables, you know how they have all those salads laid out so that when it's time to get to the main course you won't eat too much . . . that scam to get you filled up so you don't eat too much chicken and beef and all that other stuff?'

'Yeah, yeah ... I get the point,' Tilley said impatiently. 'So?'

'So I see celery, I see the lettuce, tomatoes, cauliflower ... and I think, all these things came out of the ground. They had corn – out of the ground – radish – out of the ground. You say to yourself, how can all those things come out of the ground? You know what I'm talking about? All these things are out of the ground.'

'Yeah.' Tilley nodded, though he had no idea what Sam was talking about.

'I mean, how can that be? It just happened that way? And I'm not even getting into the fruits ... I'm just dealing with the vegetables right now. With all those things coming out of the earth, there must be a God.'

Tilley looked at Sam, wondering why all of a sudden everyone was going on about the wonders of nature. First it was Nora with her damn picnics and now Sam seemed to have flipped his lid and was seeing God in a mushroom. This was the 1960s for Christ's sake, not the Middle Ages.

'I'm not getting the same religious effect that came over you,' he said. 'I don't know why, but I don't feel like running to a church to pray right this second.'

'You gotta admit, it's amazing,' Sam insisted.

'Yeah, yeah ...' Tilley agreed, growing bored with the whole subject. This was supposed to be a night off, they were here to enjoy themselves, not to talk theology. With all these broads around they should even be thinking about getting laid. He turned round to get a look at the action – and froze.

'I don't believe it,' he said thickly. 'See the guy over there.'

Sam looked across to where Tilley was pointing.

'That's the son of a bitch who crashed into my car,' Tilley growled.

'I don't believe it!' BB said, spotting Tilley at the same

moment. 'Mr Banana Head is here.'

'What?' said Moe, also turning to look.

'The crazy guy that banged into my car and smashed my windows in,' BB snarled. 'I don't fucking believe it! I'm gonna get him.'

'I'm gonna get him!' Tilley roared.

As BB and Tilley wove their way through the crowd to get to one another, the pressure of human bodies diverted their respective paths so that in the confusion they went right past each other. They turned and made for each other once more, finally meeting head to head in the middle of the room.

'You got a lot of nerve banging into my car,' BB yelled above the roar of the crowd, 'and you've got a lot of fucking nerve smashing my windows in.'

'What're you talking about?' Tilley screamed back – and lying through his teeth, 'Why would I want to break your windows?'

BB saw red. What did the schmuck take him for? 'You didn't smash my windows in?' he thundered.

'I'm a hard working guy ... I don't go around breaking windows. I've got better things to do,' Tilley stormed back, faking righteous indignation.

'You didn't break my windows!' BB raged. 'You didn't break my windows!'

He pushed Tilley backwards.

'Push me one more time and I'm gonna have to redefine your face,' Tilley screamed, bringing up his fists threateningly: BB was a few inches taller than himself but Tilley was like a raging bulldog, straining at the leash to tear Mr Marengay limb from limb.

BB pushed.

In a blind fury, Tilley threw himself at BB and as they scuffled on the floor Moe and Sam, with the help of Looney and Carly, did their best to pull them apart.

'Come on,' BB grunted as the two men were finally

separated, 'let's go outside... let's settle this in the parking lot.'

'Oh, no!' Tilley gasped. 'You're not gonna get near my car... you're not gonna kick in my headlights again –' Suddenly he remembered. 'What am I talking about? I didn't even drive tonight. You wanna duke it?' he challenged BB. 'Let's go.'

Pushing their way aggressively through the crowd they made it through the door and came out into the parking lot, looking round for some space to fight in. As they took off their jackets a crowd of people, who had followed them out of the Corral, gathered around to watch the brawl.

'What is this?' BB shouted out angrily. 'What is this crowd here? We're charging admission?'

'Back away!' Tilley snapped. 'Give me some elbow room.'

The two tin men took up exaggerated fighting stances, circling one another cautiously, looking to land the first blow. But before either one could do so Moe, hearing the sound of tires on the gravel, hissed out 'Police!'

Seconds later the police car pulled up in the lot. As one cop got out and headed into the club, the other one stayed behind in the car, watching the dispersing crowd while BB and Tilley casually leaned up against a car.

'Lucky for you the police showed,' said Tilley.

BB glared at him. 'We'll see who's the lucky one,' he spat back, picking up his coat and leaving with Moe.

Chapter Fourteen

Suddenly the typing pool in the Social Security Office was plunged into darkness, the rattling of typewriters instantly silent. Then a large cake with candles lit appeared as if out of nowhere and a huge chorus went up from all the secretaries in the pool.

'SURPRISE!'

The lights were turned on again and around a desk where a secretary – in her late twenties and very pregnant – sat smiling with embarrassment, the other secretaries had congregated.

'I never expected this,' said Ada, blushing. 'What a lovely cake.'

'Blow out the candles then,' said one of the secretaries.

Ada did her best and one of the other girls helped with the couple she missed.

'Nine candles for nine months!' someone shouted and everyone laughed.

'We'll miss you, Ada,' said another. 'You'd better bring that baby in to visit us.'

'Register him for his social security number,' said a third.

While a couple of girls handed around glasses of Coca Cola, Nora shouted out, 'I love ya, Ada, and if you're smart you won't come back.'

Now the cake was being passed around and the afternoon was quickly gathering a party atmosphere with secretaries chatting and drinking, and typewriters left unattended.

'I've just decided,' Nora said quietly to her friend, 'I'm going out with him.'

Nellie looked frankly shocked. 'You're kidding?' she whispered.

'I have to. I just want to know what it's like to be with someone else.' She took a sip of her Coke and added seriously, 'Because if what I've got with Tilley is as good as it gets, I just . . .' she shrugged her shoulders, unable to express the feeling of frustration and hopelessness she got from her present life '. . . I gotta know.'

'Well, how are you going to manage it?' Nellie asked curiously.

'Tilley doesn't get home until at least two in the morning,' Nora explained and Nellie was perturbed not to be able to detect any guilt in her friend's tone.

'I hope you know what you're doing,' she said stiffly. 'You speak to some guy at the frozen food section for five minutes . . . you could jeopardise your whole marriage.'

Nora looked sour. 'Everything I've done in my life has been safe and practical, and where's that gotten me?' She lifted her paper cup again. 'Well, here's to who knows what.'

They touched their cups.

Every exposed brick in BB's two-storey apartment bore the stamp of a confirmed bachelor, from the sparse and solidly masculine furniture, the high ceilings and austere colours – to the complete absence of a single feminine touch in the functional, unimaginative, but decent looking interior decor.

As BB and Nora danced closely in the shadows of the darkened room, Sinatra's voice came from a record player in a corner.

'In the wee small hours of the morning . . .'

On the square coffee table sat a bottle of wine and paper containers with the remains of a Chinese take-away dinner.

'I'm still nervous,' Nora whispered.

'Well, I guess that's to be expected,' BB said gently. 'You want me to take you home?'

Nora smiled. 'No, not right now.'

For a few moments they danced in silence, then BB fell into a reminiscing mood.

'Every time I listen to Sinatra, I always remember when I used to work in Atlantic City back in the late Forties . . . you know, a busboy job . . . Sinatra used to play at the 500 Club, and we used to take our dates and say, "Hey, you wanna go and hear Sinatra?" Then we'd just lean on the door of the club in the alley and listen to the music. I think the girls were looking for something a bit more uptown.'

She giggled. 'I'd go with you and lean against the door.'

They continued to dance for a few minutes, gazing at each other. Then he leaned towards her and, holding her tight, kissed her gently.

'. . . that's the time . . .' sang Sinatra, stuck in a groove, '. . . that's the time . . . that's the time . . .'

Until BB slipped off one of his loafers and, still embracing Nora, kicked it so that it hit the side of the record table. The record slipped a little and then continued to play correctly.

Nora smiled. 'You've got a pretty good aim,' she said, gazing at him.

'I sure do,' he murmured and led her towards the bedroom . . .

He waited until she was fast asleep and then slipped out of the bed, donned a robe and, taking one last look at her, crept down the stairs to the living room. Out of the pocket of his jacket which was draped over the back of a chair, he extracted a piece of paper and dialled the number.

'Yeah, he's here,' said the barman at the Pimlico Hotel. 'Just a minute... Hey, Tilley,' BB heard him calling out, 'somebody wants ya on the phone.'

Tilley, who had been sitting with Sam and some of the other tin men, got up and went over to the phone. 'Yeah, this is Tilley,' he snapped.

'Hey, asshole...' BB said quietly into the phone, 'here's the ultimate "fuck you"... I just poked your wife!'

What is this, some kind of sick joke? Tilley thought. *Maybe I'm dreaming...*

'What are you talking about?' he said into the phone.

For BB this was the best part. He could imagine how broken up the asshole must be feeling. He had it coming to him, the jerk. 'She's in my bed right now with a big smile on her face.'

Something in Tilley snapped. It was like the end of the line. 'Well, that's just fine by me,' he shouted down the phone. 'She's a pain in the ass... an albatross around my neck. You're welcome to her... keep her and may you both rot in hell!'

He slammed down the phone in fury.

BB stared at the phone, puzzled. 'Is this a set-up?' he muttered to himself. 'That son of a bitch... I bet he set me up... I thought I got him, and he got me. That son of a bitch!'

Less than ten minutes later Tilley's Cadillac tore up to the front of his house. He jumped out, slamming the door, raced up the front steps, fumbled frantically to open the door with his key; flipped on the lights, flew upstairs and began rifling through the closets and drawers, pulling out Nora's clothes, dresses, skirts, blouses, coats; opened the window wide and hurled them out into the street.

'I'm a free man!' he screamed as he tossed her underwear out of the window. 'I'm a free man!' he sang as he grabbed all her shoes and flung them onto the street. He rushed into the bathroom, gathered her toiletries in his arms and chucked them into the trash can; ran back into the bedroom and pulled a suitcase down from a shelf, tossed the trash can in the suitcase then scooped out the remaining contents of her drawers and emptied them also into the suitcase; closed the suitcase and threw that out of the window. Finally, out of breath, exhausted and sweating, he stumbled downstairs into the kitchen to get himself a drink but then he saw a pair of Nora's slippers under the kitchen table; he picked them up, opened the backdoor, tossed them outside and locked the door. Still carried along by momentum, he stood there as if a motor were running inside him. At last he walked out of the kitchen and out of the house, climbed into his car and drove away.

It was not yet two o'clock and Nora knew she still had time before Tilley got back from whatever bar he hung out in these nights. She got out of her car and started to walk towards the house when she tripped on something in the street.

Looking down, her mouth fell open and she gave a little shriek as she took in the sight of all her clothing, shoes, coats, underwear and toiletries scattered over the lawn and sidewalk: panties lay on hedges; perfumes in the flowerbeds.

'Oh, my God!' she whispered, reeling from the shock.

Unable to think straight, she just stood there, as tears streamed down her face, surrounded by the remnants of her ruined marriage.

*

To BB, it was like the bullet of a gun he had fired at a steel target had richocheted back into his stomach.

'... He must have gone crazy,' Nora wailed as she stood once more at his front door with a suitcase in her hand. 'I don't know what happened to him... he must have found out I was with you... I don't know... I don't know what to do...'

She burst into tears and reached out for him to hug her.

'Can I stay with you for a day or two?' she sobbed as BB put his arms round her comfortingly.

'Sure,' he mumbled hoarsely, wondering what had hit him.

Chapter Fifteen

'Hello, this is Gibraltar Aluminum Siding Company,' declaimed a telephone girl as Tilley walked through from the pool hall to the back offices, 'we're taking a survey . . .'

'. . . Would you be interested in our field representative giving you a home demonstration?' a second girl was saying.

'. . . home demonstration,' continued a third canvasser. 'We will have some factory representatives in your area today as it happens.'

'Tilley!' called out Wing from a far office, 'let me see you.'

He rubbed a hand across his head, nursing a lethal hangover. 'Wing, give me a minute to get a cup of coffee here,' he shouted back and walked over to the coffee machine, passing Sam on the way.

'What about Super Highway in the seventh,' Sam was saying to Mouse and Gil as he looked through the sports page of his newspaper. 'It's paying seven to one. Ran well in its last race.'

'Super Highway . . .' Gil mused.

'Four in the fourth,' Tilley called out to Sam, 'twenty bucks.'

'Who's that?' Sam asked looking down the columns.

'I don't know . . . it just came to me – number four in the fourth.'

'Number four in the fourth?' Sam looked up at Tilley.

'Rider's Revenge – sixty to one, never been in the money. Nice pick, Tilley. Why don't you just throw the twenty dollars in the trash can right now.'

'Rider's Revenge . . .' Tilley repeated. 'I like that name. I've gotta go and see Wing.'

Sam was staring at him in a peculiar way, maybe thinking he was losing his marbles. Well, he hadn't felt so sane in a long long while. He was free and it felt kind of strange, like he was freewheeling and things could be opening up for him. Marengay really had done him a favor. He should have walked out on Nora years ago. In any case, there was no going back on it now. He had to stand up and show what kind of a man he was, show some guts. Sometimes you just had to roll with the dice.

'Look,' he said irritably, 'we can be scientific from now to Doomsday, but we gotta be gutsy and go for the big one.'

Sam, Gil and Mouse stared after him as he went through the door into Wing's office – which was as casual, if not downright messy, as everything else in the Gibraltar offices.

As Tilley closed the door, his coffee, which was filled to the top of the paper cup, spilled over the top and scalded his hand.

'Ah!' he shrieked, jumping back and putting the coffee down on a desk, then he wiped his hand on the back of his jacket.

'What's up, Wing?' he snapped.

'You lost a sale, Tilley. The Hudsons' loan didn't go through.'

Tilley frowned. 'What do ya mean? They wouldn't clear the loan?'

Wing pulled out a letter from the pile of papers that cluttered his desk. 'This Mr Hudson's some guy,' he said drily. 'He's got three outstanding shoplifting charges, failure to pay child support from a previous marriage . . .

guy's overdue on his mortgage, overdue on his car loan and was fired from his last job for misappropriation of funds.'

'What's wrong with the world?' said Tilley angrily. 'There are sick people out there! Thievin' son of a bitch like that takes up my time... cuts into the amount of hours I have available to deal with other people interested in my wares! There's no fuckin' sympathy for the working man in this country.'

'They don't make our job easy, Tilley.'

'Wing, it was such a beautiful thing,' Tilley said regretfully. 'You shoulda seen how I worked. Like a magician... "This job is free"! It was my best... my best! There's no fucking justice in this world... there ain't no justice.'

He sighed and picked up his coffee.

'Did you see the paper?' said Wing casually.

'What section?'

'Take a look at this.' He passed the *Baltimore Sun* over the desk.

'"Home Improvement Commission..."' Tilley muttered. '"Hearings begin today..." Is this McCarthyism?' he said indignantly, refolding the paper. What are they gonna see? If there are any communists?'

'Just cool down the scams, okay Tilley?' Wing said calmly.

Tilley shrugged.

It was an unprepossessing location to hold major State Hearings but until something more substantial could be worked out the tobacco warehouse would be the temporary headquarters for the Commission. Amidst boxes and crates, a number of tables had been grouped together to form one long table behind which a number of Commissioners were seated. The Defense table was situated a few yards across the room.

Presiding over the Hearings was John Masters, a seedy-looking man in his late forties with dark rings under his eyes, who smoked incessantly. He had removed his jacket and undone the top button of his shirt to loosen his tie, and the Home Improvement Commissioners who sat to his left and right were no less sloppily dressed.

An array of hastily and clumsily rigged microphones and sound booms echoed Masters' voice off the walls and creates, projecting it across to a small gallery of journalists and other interested onlookers.

He cleared his throat as he continued to interrogate a weasel-faced tin man in his early forties.

'Now, when you made your initial sales pitch, did you indicate that you would be giving free storm windows with the job?'

There was a slight pause as Murray Banks worked up an answer.

'Free storm windows?' Banks finally said, leaning into the microphone.

'Yes,' Masters snapped impatiently. 'That you would provide a free set of storm windows with the sale of aluminum siding.'

An ugly sound reverberated around the warehouse as Banks also cleared his throat.

'No, sir,' he replied impassively. 'I wouldn't be able to make any money if I was giving away storm windows. My cost of a storm window is somewhere like –'

Masters cut him off wearily. 'The point being that you had no intention of giving away the storm windows.'

At the back of the warehouse BB and Moe stood by the door anxiously listening to the Hearings.

'The storm windows, as I can recall, was not an issue,' Banks replied carefully. 'I mentioned that I thought the storm windows would cut down on their heating bill, and that they would obviously enhance the look of the house with the aluminum siding work we were going to do.'

'So you weren't dangling a free set of storm windows as a come-on to selling them the aluminum siding job?' Masters pressed him. 'Because it says here, and I'm reading from a statement from Mr Tabaleri...'

'What do ya make of all this?' Moe whispered.

BB looked grave. 'It's the future, Moe... it's the future.'

'"It was my understanding,"' Masters read from Tabaleri's statement, '"that the storm windows were included in the price of the sale..."'

Moe and BB had heard enough.

'Where do you think they're getting this information from?' said Moe as they walked back to BB's new Cadillac – he'd managed to negotiate a 'loaner' from the dealership though he fully intended that Tilley would be footing the bill for the damage, or, if necessary, a brand new model.

'I dunno,' BB replied uneasily. 'Looks like any tin man gets in that hot seat, then he's had it.'

Moe whistled. 'Then they can take your license forever... it don't seem fair.'

They walked past a Volkswagon Beetle parked in front of BB's Cadillac.

'Boy, I tell ya, I bet you could sell a ton of these things,' said BB, intrigued.

'That?' Moe shook his head. 'Too silly looking.'

For a few more seconds, BB continued to gaze at the Volkswagon, as if entranced, then walked on to his own car.

'Ever see a dealership?' he said offhandedly.

'No.'

'Interesting,' said BB as something began to stir in his mind.

Chapter Sixteen

'I keep racking my brain. I gotta get find a way to really get even with this guy.'

Tilley was sitting at a table with Sam at the Pimlico Race Track Turf Club. While Sam studied the racing form, Tilley was pretending to study the menu but he was finding it impossible to concentrate.

'It isn't enough to wreck his car . . .' he said pensively. 'Even breaking into his house and messing it up or something, that don't have enough impact. I mean, the man poked my wife! I gotta come up with something ingenious . . . something ingenious.'

Sam noticed the waiter approaching and silently gestured to Tilley to change the subject.

'So, what do ya think?' he said as the waiter hovered.

Tilley deliberated. 'I think I'll take some meatloaf.'

'Meatloaf,' the waiter repeated, writing it down.

'No, I think I'll have some fish,' Tilley corrected himself.

The waiter crossed out 'meatloaf' and began writing 'fish', but Tilley changed his mind again.

'No, no . . . fish doesn't fill you up. Meatloaf.' He closed the menu.

'So, it's meatloaf?' the waiter said patiently.

'What do you think,' Sam said to Tilley, looking up from the racing form. 'Sally's Pride in the second? Get me a Bloody Mary,' he added to the waiter.

'Anything other than the Bloody Mary?' the waiter asked him.

'What number is Sally's Pride?' Tilley said.

'Six,' Sam replied, and turned back to the waiter. 'No, I don't like to eat until the third race.'

The waiter walked off.

'Six . . . six . . . six . . . six,' Tilley pondered, putting his hand to his brow, then shook his head. 'I'm thinking "one". Who's number one?'

Sam checked the form. 'Mr Motor.'

'Then that's it,' Tilley said firmly. 'I'm going with number one.'

Sam put down the form. 'Tilley, this is insane,' he said in a vexed tone. 'You're picking horses because you think you're clairvoyant or something.'

'Sam, I'm not doing too well by checking the stats, so why not. I put my hand to my forehead, I see a one – Mr Motor in the second . . . twenty bucks.'

They looked towards the track as the horses raced to the finishing line, Number nine was in the lead and streaked across the line.

'Hallihan's Daughter,' Sam announced.

Tilley couldn't contain himself. 'I got it!' he laughed, 'I got it!' He picked up the racing form. 'Seven to one . . . hundred and forty smackers.' He laughed again with satisfaction. 'Hand to the forehead! Hand to the forehead!'

Sam remained unconvinced. 'You're not talking about a longshot. Mr Motor, for instance, is coming off at fifty to one.'

Tilley wasn't listening. He had closed his eyes and was again tapping his forehead. 'Third race, I see a six . . . I see a three. I don't think the verdict's in on that one yet.'

He stood up and went through his money and race tickets. 'Wing paid a hundred on number five, he loses, I got hundred and fifty . . . next race, I'll lay down the bet.'

He glanced quickly at Sam. 'What you taking in this race?'

'Thrifty's Delight – number four . . . twenty bucks.'

Tilley thought for a second. 'You take Thrifty's Delight – twenty bucks, I got twenty on Mr Motor, Wing's got a hundred on Night Fire.' He looked over at the form. 'What's the odds on Night Fire?'

'Twenty to one.'

'I don't see Night Fire winning,' Tilley said and then came to a decision. 'Fuck it, I'm not gonna even place the bet . . . I just made a hundred bucks.'

Sam stared at him. 'What are you, crazy? What happens if he wins?'

'He's not gonna win . . . I feel it,' Tilley replied tapping his forehead one more time as he headed towards the betting booths.

On his way there he caught sight of Wing entering the race track. 'Hey, Wing,' he yelled, 'we're sitting just off the left of the entrance. I'm gonna lay down your bet right now. See you in a minute. You lost the first race in case you don't know.'

BB had more on his mind to worry about than just the Commission or even Tilley. Nora was already beginning to get on his nerves.

'I tell you something, she's getting on my nerves,' he said as he drove across town to follow up another lead.

'Who, Nora?' said Moe.

'Yeah, yeah . . . who else is it gonna be . . . "Who, Nora!" . . . who else is there?' He drove in silence for a few seconds but then, unable to leave the subject hanging in the air, went on, 'The whole idea of being with a girl on consecutive nights is new to me. It's one thing when they're with you for a night, but when they live with ya, it's stretching the point. They got a lot of things they bring with them . . . you go to the bathroom, you see "things" you never saw before.'

Moe shrugged. 'So what's the to do?'

'Well, they move their stuff around and it's not where it used to be . . . I'm not used to that.'

Moe looked at him in surprise. 'You mean all this time you've never lived with a girl?'

'What!' BB exclaimed. 'Did we just meet? How long we been partners? No, I've never lived with a girl!'

His face was as white as a sheet and he had to swerve to avoid crashing into the car in front. He muttered a curse. Two crashes in one week would be some joke.

'Boy oh boy!' Moe grinned. 'Did you wake up on the wrong side of the bed today?'

'Yes, I did,' BB said angrily. 'I came in last night, she was sleeping on my side of the bed. In my life I never got out of bed on the left side . . . in my life never from the left.' He gazed out of the car window. 'I got close once up in the Catskills. I met this girl, Dorian. For a week we were together, but it wasn't the same because she always went to her room to change and do all that stuff. She didn't have things in my room.'

He gave a deep, weary sigh. 'All this, 'cos I'm trying to get even with some guy.'

It occurred to Moe that if BB was thinking straight he'd have put an end to this straight away, before he got in too deep.

'You know what?' BB said. 'I think I got to see her and put an end to this.'

Chapter Seventeen

This time the secretaries at the Social Security Office were hard at work and when BB peeked his head round the corner and walked into the office he felt highly conspicuous. As he made his way along the long line of desks searching for Nora he received curious glances from the hundreds of secretaries and clerks who were typing or doing paperwork.

Nellie looked up from her typewriter to see a man in a thick overcoat looking rather lost as he wandered towards them. It was obvious that he was looking for someone and on a hunch, she whispered to Nora, 'Is that him?'

Nora looked up and saw him. 'Yes,' she said, smiling. 'Bill!' she yelled out.

BB turned towards her and she waved, happily, with an affectionate twinkle in her eye.

'Yeah,' he said faintly, giving her a self-conscious little wave as the whole department turned to stare at him.

'I'm glad you stopped by,' Nora said giving him a little kiss as they sat down together in the coffee area. 'This is a real surprise.'

'Listen,' BB launched in straightaway, 'I got a problem.'

Her eyes widened. 'Oh. How can I help?'

She looked so trusting. He really did have a problem.

'Um . . . er . . .' he began. This was going to be hard:

she clearly didn't have the faintest idea what this was about. 'Well, the problem is . . . like . . . is like . . . er, you know . . . you're the problem.'

Nora's eyes widened even more. 'Really,' she said softly. 'How so?'

It was time to talk straight. 'There's things that are bothering me,' he said wretchedly.

'Like what?'

'You know . . . things.'

'Things?'

BB sighed. Was she deliberately giving him a hard time?

'You know, like things that come up . . .' he stuttered, 'stuff . . . like . . . you know, annoyances.'

'Annoyances?' She looked puzzled.

'Hard to explain,' he mumbled, feeling like a heel. 'Very hard.'

'Well, try.'

BB took a deep breath. 'As an example . . . I came home last night, I get undressed, and I realise you're sleeping on my side of the bed. I've always slept on that side . . . it's something I've always done.'

She looked amused. 'Then why didn't you just nudge me a bit and tell me to go and sleep on the other side?'

'I didn't want to wake you up,' he said sheepishly. 'I thought you might think it was kind of stupid or something.'

'Well,' she smiled, 'that's easily changed.'

This wasn't going the way he'd planned. 'But there are other things . . .' he tried again, 'bigger things.' He gazed at her green eyes and once again lost his nerve. 'I realise just talking about it, they all sound petty and silly.'

Nora put her hand on his arm, 'Listen,' she said gently, 'if you think all of this is going too fast, maybe I should move out. Is that what you want, Bill?'

BB shifted in his seat and looked around, feeling very

uncomfortable. He shrugged noncommittally.

'I really care for you,' she went on, 'but if you think it's best.'

He looked wretched.

'I don't want to make you unhappy,' she added.

'I don't think we've got to take drastic action,' he mumbled.

Nora smiled, relieved.

'Thought I'd come by and get things off my chest . . .' BB concluded weakly, 'talk it out.'

He looked at her for a moment. 'Listen, I'm going over to Pimlico . . . catch the seventh race . . . wanna come?'

She shook her head reluctantly. 'I can't get away from work.'

'I know.'

He started to walk away, then turned back and gave her a quick kiss. Nora watched his huddled figure recede as he walked away through the rows and rows of secretaries.

Tilley had reached a fever pitch of excitement as the race drew to a climax. 'We're taking a thirty to one shot,' he yelled. 'Number eight . . . come on number eight . . . Streamers . . . come on you sucker!'

Beside him in the Turf Club, Sam and Wing watched quietly as Streamers, still in the lead, came around the home stretch.

'Thirty to one,' Tilley screamed. 'A hundred bucks on you, number eight. There's a guy up here who put a hundred on ya. Come on . . . come on . . . come on, baby . . . come on baby!'

Seconds later, his face fell: at the last moment, another horse, number fourteen, overtook Streamers to race past the winning post.

'Nooooooo!' Tilley groaned.

Wing smiled. 'I've got myself a winner,' he said

quietly.

Tilley, realising what he'd done, turned to look at Wing, just as Sam turned towards Tilley, with obvious concern on his face.

In the grandstand, BB grinned as the totals flashed on the board, indicating that the winning horse paid $16.30.

'Way to go . . .' he beamed triumphantly at Moe. 'Southern Belle.'

Moe tore up his ticket in disgust.

'Should have bet with me, Moe,' BB said smugly.

Meanwhile in the Turf Club Wing was calculating his winnings. 'Very nice!' he smiled.

'That was your horse, Wing?' Tilley asked casually, hoping against hope that Wing might have forgotten.

'Yeah . . . Southern Belle,' Wing replied amiably. 'You oughta know, you bet her for me.'

Tilley had turned green. 'Of course,' he swallowed.

'I'm gonna go with the favorite in this one,' said Wing, consulting the form, 'Fordnee Lane. I tell you what, I won sixteen plus on the other race. From those winnings you can bet me eight hundred.'

'Eight hundred?' Tilley echoed, going paler by the second.

'Yeah . . . I wanna bet eight hundred on Fordnee Lane.'

'Fordnee Lane – eight hundred,' Tilley repeated helplessly. 'Eight hundred.'

Sam gazed at him pityingly, aware that he was now in a real jam.

'Waiter, can you get me a cup of coffee,' Wing called out as Tilley stared back in panic at Sam.

'You guys want anything else?' said Wing to Sam and Tilley before the waiter departed.

Sam shook his head.

'No,' said Tilley, nodding, 'Er . . . hum . . . er . . . hey, Wing . . . I tell you, I got a problem.'

'What is it?' said Wing, who was in a magnanimous mood.

'It's the eight hundred on Fordnee Lane,' Tilley said nervously. 'I haven't got it.'

Wing chuckled. 'No, you got it wrong. You take it from the sixteen plus I won . . . the eight hundred.'

'I haven't got the winnings,' said Tilley, staring at his boss fixedly.

'What do ya mean, you don't have the winnings,' Wing said angrily.

'Wing, it was the craziest thing,' Tilley began to babble, 'I didn't want to mention it earlier because it was so nuts . . . it was the craziest thing.'

'What?'

Tilley giggled. 'I don't know how to even tell you this without being embarrassed for myself. It was an accident . . . it's like one of those things out of the blue . . . it's crazy . . . you can't explain something like this . . . it just happens.'

Wing stared sternly at Tilley, then turned to Sam. 'What is he talking about?'

'He had an accident of some sort,' Sam said quietly.

By now Tilley was wriggling around like a worm on a hotplate. 'It happens . . . I don't know how . . . I don't know how to explain. It's too crazy, I swear to God, Wing.'

His boss put a hand up to silence him. 'Wait a minute,' he said stonily, 'You're telling me that I didn't win the last race?'

Tilley laughed again nervously. 'You won, Wing . . . you won, it's just that you're not getting any money . . . it was a fluke. I swear, I don't know how it could have happened. A ten year old couldn't have made the mistake I made . . . I don't know, I swear.'

Wing was losing patience. 'What the fuck is he talking about?' he said to Sam.

'If there was some way I could make it up,' Tilley persisted, 'believe me, I would, because you know where I stand.'

For a moment Wing just stared at Tilley as the truth dawned on him.

'You know where I stand, Wing,' Tilley blathered on, like he was on a rollercoaster. 'If there was any way, believe me, I'd make it up. I'd give you thirty percent of what you didn't get because it was a fluke . . . I'm willing to make some kind of retribution.'

Wing was black with fury. 'You just pocketed the goddamned money,' he growled. 'You just took my money and slipped it into your goddamned pocket, didn't you?'

'No,' Tilley went on dementedly. 'I'd split fifty-fifty with you, that's how badly I feel, under the circumstances.'

Wing grabbed Tilley by his tie and collar. 'You get this straight, you son of a bitch,' he snarled, 'you owe me sixteen plus . . . I want sixteen plus.'

He released the quivering tin man who backed away slightly, lifting his hands in a gesture of surrender.

'Am I trying to shirk my responsibility?' he gasped. 'That's not the way I see it . . . it was a fluke, a crazy thing that happened, but I stand behind my honor on this . . . put it on my tab.'

Wing's anger had given way to intense frustration and bewilderment. 'What the hell is wrong with him?' he turned in desperation to Sam. 'What the hell is wrong with him? He's stealing money from me . . . what the hell is wrong with him? Can you tell me?'

Sam chickened out. 'I don't know the whole story,' he said feebly.

'You work with him, Sam . . . for Christ sake . . .' Wing persisted.

'What do you mean, wrong?' Tilley said indignantly,

trying to regain some dignity. 'It was a fluke . . . it was an accident. I don't know what the hell went wrong. It was a one in a million thing that happened to me when I went to place that bet. I'm trying to do what I can.'

Wing could only look at him sadly and shake his head. 'Tilley,' he sighed, 'what the hell happened to you?'

Chapter Eighteen

Sam was mad with Tilley but he waited until they'd parted ways with Wing and were leaving the race track before he brought up the subject.

'Why didn't you at least give him the six hundred that you pocketed from the six races he lost?'

'Fuck him!' Tilley said with more complacence than malice. 'It's on my tab. I've got six hundred in my pocket right now. It's like another loan. Sam, you got to think about today. Today, I got six hundred bucks in my pocket. You know what I'm saying?'

Sam rolled his eyes. 'Yeah,' he said, getting the point only too well.

'It's like some guy trying to sell me life insurance. You think I'm gonna take some money out of my pocket to give to some jerk so that somebody can take it when I'm dead? No, Sam, you gotta live for today. I'm gonna live as good as I can every day. You know what I'm saying?'

They were approaching Tilley's Cadillac just as BB and Moe were walking towards BB's Cadillac. Tilley reacted first.

'Hey, Mr Marengay went to the track!' he yelled.

'Did you bother to bet,' BB flung back, 'or did you just hand your money to the tellers?'

'The sarcasm's killing me,' Tilley faked a laugh. 'I thought you were looking to get even.'

'Who's your accountant, mister, 'cos I think you're down in the debit side.'

Tilley really laughed this time. 'Who's stuck with my wife? You or me?'

BB stared at him. 'You want me to believe that you were setting me up with your wife as some kind of decoy?'

'Decoy is the word!' Tilley sneered.

For a long moment the two tin men eyed one another, then, softly, almost apologetically, BB murmured, 'Okay then, you win.'

He turned on his heel and got into his car.

Tilley gazed after him. 'I win?' he repeated in astonishment. 'That guy would never let me win. He must be setting me up. The son of a bitch is setting me up, Sam.'

His partner was fast losing patience with Tilley. 'For crying out loud, why don't you just leave at that... you win.'

Tilley shook his head. 'I couldn't have won,' he said firmly. 'I smell a rat.'

He looked back at BB's car which was pulling away.

Inside the car, Moe couldn't help letting his partner know he was proud of him.

'BB, I think you're getting a little humility in your blood.'

'If getting Nora is part of losing,' BB replied in a strange voice, 'Thank God I didn't win.'

Moe started with surprise. Could it be that for the first time ever – so far as Moe was aware – Bill Babowski had fallen for a broad?

The section of the old tobacco warehouse which had not been converted into the HQ for the Commission Hearings had instead been turned into a makeshift office for the Home Improvement Commission, with desks, chairs and filing cabinets stacked on top of each other and cartons and boxes piled high against the walls.

The Commission was just getting into gear and with the info they were getting from Stanley Franks it was going to make all their lives a lot easier.

'This is good, Stan . . . nice work,' John Masters said, throwing the file down on a table where Stanley was seated with his feet up, nursing a hot cup of coffee.

Stanley nodded modestly.

'Fossey says it should go down very well with the City Council,' Masters went on. 'Could help us appropriate more funds. This goes a long way to establish our credibility in what we're trying to do.'

'There's a lot more where this came from,' said Stanley, having to raise his voice above the deafening noise of sawing, hammering and electric drills.

'You know what I think you should do now,' Masters suggested. 'Why don't you pull some files . . . some files that were completed, others that went unsold, and I'll have somebody run it down, talk to the customers and get some statements.'

Stanley looked doubtful. 'Pulling files is another thing. That might not be easy.'

'You could just sneak a few here and there when you can.'

'I'll see,' Stanley said cautiously.

'I think that might be good,' Masters smiled.

Moe and BB were doing the showcase hustle.

'What do you think if we made this one of our factory showcase houses?' Moe asked BB over Mr Shubner's head.

'What's that?' Shubner said curiously.

It's a good location,' BB said to Moe. 'Get a lot of traffic on the street.'

'What does that mean, Mr Gable?' Shubner asked Moe again.

'You know what I do, Alan?' Moe said confidentially.

'I pick certain houses that are strategically located, we put up the aluminum siding, and for every referral, for every person who sees this quality job that we do – sees how beautiful it is – I give you two hundred dollars.'

'Two hundred dollars?' Shubner was visibly impressed and so was his wife. They were a young couple and all this was new to them. That's why Moe had picked them out for this particular scam.

'That's right,' said Moe with a grin. 'God knows how many houses we could sell by people passing this house. It's perfectly placed for that.'

Ostentatiously he took out his wallet. 'Alan, this is how confident I feel that this house will drum up business for me.' He peeled off four hundred dollars and handed the money to Shubner who stared at it, unable to believe his good fortune.

'Four hundred dollars,' Moe went on. 'I'm giving you commission on two house referrals before I put a panel on the side of your house . . . that's how confident I feel.'

It seemed too good to be true, and Shubner was having last-minute doubts. 'You think that many people are going to –'

'I'm certain of it,' Moe interrupted him. 'I'm not giving away four hundred dollars for my health . . . I'm a businessman, and I'm a good businessman. This is good business for me. I'm giving it away 'cos I believe in this house, believe that it will refer me to other jobs which means money in my pocket – which means money in your pocket.'

Shubner was satisfied and so was his wife. 'You got a deal, Mr Gable,' he smiled, shaking hands with both tin men.

Suddenly, Moe winced in pain and clasped a hand to his chest.

'Something wrong, sir?' said Shubner.

The next moment Moe collapsed to the floor.

Chapter Nineteen

As a couple of nursing attendants wheeled Moe on a gurney along the endless hospital corridor, BB anxiously walked alongside.

'I finally got hold of May,' he told Moe, 'she was over at your sister's.'

'Oh, I forgot,' Moe replied, breathing heavily and painfully.

'She'll be down here shortly,' BB went on, hoping Moe didn't pick up on the shock he was feeling.

Moe's heart attack had affected BB more than he could have imagined. Moe Gable wasn't just a partner – he'd been like a father and a brother and a friend. It wasn't something BB liked to think too much about: tin men weren't the kind of guys who made a big deal of these things but when you'd been in some of the situations BB and Moe had been in, when the mark was going cold on the deal and you couldn't rely on any of the old scams, then a kind of telepathy built up between you, so you knew what your partner was going to say and do next like it was yourself doing it.

Besides this, something was happening in BB's life that was entirely unexpected and he still didn't know how to deal with it and it had everything to do with Nora. Funny thing was, the saying went that tin men didn't have hearts and here was Moe about to have heart surgery and here he was unable to get her out of his mind. He couldn't figure out how it had happened: she wasn't glamorous, she wasn't a looker – at least he hadn't thought so when he'd first set eyes on her in the supermarket and only a few days ago he was sounding off to Moe about how he couldn't deal with a woman like that in his life but now, tonight, even walking down this corridor, he couldn't wait to see her. And he no longer cared which side of the bed she slept on just as long as she was in it.

He thought he'd had the complete package, the whole armor-plated defence against such an invasion and now he realised that he had no defences at all. What he couldn't get out of his mind was how she could have been married to a shmuck like Tilley. She was like . . . he gave up, there was no one like her.

'You okay Moe?' he asked gently.

'BB,' Moe gasped, 'I don't have any insurance. If I die, May's got nothing . . . nothing . . . nothing for Leonard. The only money I've got is in my pocket. That's all I got.'

Please God this doesn't happen to me, BB thought. 'Just take it easy, Moe,' he said. 'Rest.'

'Did they sign?' Moe gasped. 'Did they sign?'

'Don't worry about it now.'

'God damn it, BB! Did you sign them?'

He was trying to shout but it came out in an almost incoherent wheeze.

'Don't worry . . . don't worry,' BB said, trying not to raise his own voice. 'I'll take care of it tomorrow.'

'God damn,' Moe panted, 'my chest hurts . . . I always taught you, BB, never walk out of a place without a signed contract. Somebody's word ain't spit.'

'They'll sign, Moe. Don't worry, they'll sign.'

He rang her from a public phone in the hospital hallway. He couldn't wait to hear her voice.

'This is kind of new to me,' he said a little sheepishly,

'but I thought I better call and tell you I'm gonna be late . . . maybe two or three. I never had anyone there to call before, but I thought I should call, you know.'

'Why? Do you think you have some obligation?'

It was hard to tell if she was teasing him or not. She kept knocking him sideways.

'I dunno,' he mumbled. 'I thought I'd better call, that's all.'

'Well, I'm glad you did,' said Nora.

There was a slight pause.

'I don't know what's gonna happen to Moe,' he said, suddenly feeling very lonely.

'Well, I hope he's okay . . . I'll see you when you get in.' She blew a kiss down the phone.

'Yeah,' BB said, looking at the receiver.

He hung up and walked across to the ward. Through the glass door he could see Moe lying beneath an oxygen tent.

The Gibraltar tin men had just finished breakfast in their usual diner. It was time for the reckoning.

'Let me see what the damage is,' said Sam, reaching for the bill. He hummed as he read it. 'Babum . . . babum . . . babum . . . babum . . . Mouse, figure it out, will ya?' he said, handing the bill across the table.

'Why don't we just split it five ways?' said Gil.

'No way!' Tilley protested. 'I didn't eat anything, so why should I pay for Mouse . . . he eats like an animal.'

'Well, sometimes you'll eat more than he does, and it'll even out,' Sam pointed out.

But Tilley was adamant. 'No way!' he repeated. 'He's a pig! He always eats more than anyone else. Why should I pay for his food?'

'What're you talking about?' Mouse complained. 'Today I happened to have eggs and flapjacks, some cantalope, some juice and then another juice.'

Tilley nodded vigorously. It proved his point. 'Like an animal! Like an animal!'

Mouse held his hand up. 'But yesterday, what did I have?'

'What did he have?' Tilley tried to recall. 'Sam, what did he have?'

Sam yawned. 'Let me get out my notebook. How the fuck do I know what he had?'

Tilley shrugged. 'Well, I don't remember what he had. Gil, what did he have?'

'Pancakes?' Gil suggested.

Mouse shook his head like a slow windshield wiper. 'No.'

'Then what did you have?' Tilley demanded.

'Guess,' said Mouse, enjoying this.

'What is this, a quiz show?' Tilley growled. 'We don't know what you had. What did you have?'

Mouse hesitated.

'I had very little,' he answered finally.

'Very little!' Tilley roared. 'You eat like an animal! It couldn't have been very little.'

'I didn't have that much...' Mouse declared positively, then he turned to the assembled company either appealing for support or demanding the correct answer like a teacher in first grade – it was hard to tell which, on account of Mouse's talent for being hard to read which made him such a bastard to play poker with.

'Doesn't anybody remember?'

'We don't remember,' Sam gave the consensus view. 'I don't know why.'

Gil was looking stunned as though his memory was an old trusted friend who had let him down.

'I could have sworn he had pancakes,' he said faintly.

'He said he didn't have pancakes,' Tilley snarled, growing angrier by the minute.

'I'll give you a clue,' Mouse said generously. 'Maple

syrup was used.'

'That's what I'm saying,' Gil said excitedly. 'It was pancakes like I said.'

'I don't give a shit,' Tilley fumed.

'French toast,' Sam suggested.

There was a knock on the window of the diner.

'French toast?' Tilley rejoined the battle. 'He had more than French toast.'

'Yes, but not a lot more,' Mouse modified.

The knocking on the window increased.

Tilley had really had enough of this. 'I don't give a damn,' he muttered. 'It's split five ways.'

Gil nudged him. 'Your wife's knocking on the window.'

Tilley looked across to the window: it was Nora. He pointed to the far end of the diner. She nodded and began walking to the front door. It was an encounter neither of them were looking forward to.

'Was not long ago you never would have seen a woman in here,' Tilley said a little stiltedly.

They were drinking toffee at a table away from the other tin men. Nora ran her eyes dispiritedly around the place. Workmen sat staring vacantly ahead of them. An old Connie Francis record was playing on the jukebox. The pervasive smell of frying, disinfectant and stale tobacco smoke; the windows permanently steamed up; the shuffling of men's shoes and boots, and someone's incessant coughing, the grind of the coffee machine, the occasional humorless laugh and frequent swearing... she hated it maybe more than she hated anything else in this world.

'You don't have to tell me,' she said sourly. 'How many nights did you drop me off and come up here all the time?'

Tilley sighed. They'd had this conversation how many

times? He'd lost count.

'I know,' he said quietly. 'I was just trying to be congenial . . . you know, start a conversation off, on a nice kind of light level, you know.' He glanced at her. She looked kind of different – younger. She still had a good shape, she could still turn a few heads – like Marengay's. Well, they were welcome to each other. All he knew was he'd tried to do his best, tried to earn a living for them both and where had it got him? From now on he'd be looking after number one, it was the only way . . .

'So, what's the scoop, Nora?' he said calmly.

She looked nervous, flushed. 'Well, you know, I think we really should get divorced,' she said quickly.

He shrugged. 'Makes sense. You want some more coffee?'

Nora looked up at him, disconcerted. Did he really feel so little, or was he pretending?

'Yeah, I'll have some,' she said.

'Florence,' Tilley shouted over to the waitress, 'some coffee here.' He turned back to Nora. 'It's for the best . . . You know, we were kind of fooling ourselves, weren't we?'

'Yes,' she said, feeling oddly relieved and sad at the same time. It was like she was talking to a complete stranger: they had nothing in common, except the years they'd wasted together. 'It went wrong somewhere along the line – I don't know where though.'

Tilley nodded. Funny thing was, this was the first time for as long as he could remember he'd been able to sit down with Nora and just talk. Why hadn't they done this before? Maybe if they could talk more like this, maybe . . .

'Yes, something went wrong . . . I don't know.' He stopped as Florence walked over and poured them coffee.

They drank it in silence for half a minute.

'So you like this guy?' he said stiffly.

'Yeah, I like him.'

Tilley nodded. She liked the guy. Well, that was none of his business.

'All in all I guess it'll all work out for the best,' he said.

'I'm glad you feel that way.'

'Yeah, can you figure it out?' he smiled philosophically. 'A guy bangs into my car, thinks I did him in, tries to get even with me by stealing my wife, you two people fall in love . . . can you figure that out?'

She stared at him, at first not making sense of what he was saying. Was he really so broken up that he was confusing two people he had a grudge against, thinking they were the same person? No, she decided, he wasn't that broken up. In that case . . .

'What?' she said, turning pale.

Tilley looked at her in astonishment. 'You telling me you didn't know this was the guy?'

'This was *that* guy?' she said faintly.

'Yeah, I told you I ran into another tin man.'

Nora had gone rigid. 'He didn't tell me he was a tin man . . . he told me he sold baby pictures.'

Tilley shrugged. 'It's your life. All I know is this guy has a bent weather vane.'

She stared through him in horror. It was like her worst nightmare had come true.

'Oh, God!' she said tonelessly. 'Not another tin man.'

Chapter Twenty

'Good afternoon, this is Superior Aluminum Siding. We're going to have...'

'... a salesman in your area today...'

It should have been business as usual at Superior but, for BB, Moe's absence made the office feel like a morgue.

'Beeb,' said Looney as they sat in the back office, 'why don't you let Stanley work with you. I'm off to Florida at the end of the week for some sun and fun. Let Stanley work with you, and when I get back, we'll see how Moe's doing.'

BB didn't like the idea. 'I don't know,' he said dubiously. 'To be honest with you, I think I'd rather work alone... he's too green. Is he a pain in the ass?'

Looney blinked a few times, considering this. 'No,' he decided. 'He don't talk much; he's a good listener, so he can't really get on your nerves. He's a lousy pool player and he can't play cards for shit, but –'

'So what good is he?' BB interrupted him.

Looney once again pondered. 'Studious type,' he said finally. 'Takes a lot of notes.'

BB grinned, shaking his head. 'If this is a sales pitch, I think you got to work a little harder 'cos I don't think you've got good product.'

Looney started to twitch.

Studious type... takes a lot of notes...

BB frowned to himself as he walked out of the

Superior Aluminum building and headed for his car. Something didn't smell right about Stanley. What was a guy like that – with his college education – doing selling tin? Maybe he was being unreasonably suspicious: after all, he'd been in the same position himself in the early Fifties in a manner of speaking – he'd gone from being a street-vendor and busboy in Atlantic City to an out-of-work actor off Broadway and no one said there was no room for actors in the tin game... well, maybe Moe helped to rub a few sharp corners off him but the point was no one said he didn't have a right to do the job, so he shouldn't go judging Stanley now. Even so, BB knew one thing: Stanley might shape up in time but he'd have to throw away his notebook. What a tin man needed to know was in his head and in his guts.

He had nearly reached his baby blue Cadillac (which he had reclaimed from the local mechanic the previous day) and was about to get in when he was startled by the screech of car tyres. He looked up in time to see Nora in her old Chevy, a few yards in front of him, driving it forward and then suddenly reversing it hard into his car.

'What are you, crazy?' he shouted, running over towards her.

But she was doing it again: she drove her car forward and then backwards again, this time almost running BB himself down. Then she rolled down the window and yelled, 'You're a goddamn tin man!'

Again she backed her car up as BB tried to get round the front of it to talk to her.

'Wait a minute!' he shouted frantically. 'Wait a minute!'

Once more she started to move the car towards him and he was only just in time to dodge out of the way, instead the Chevy smashed into the side of his car.

'You wanted to win me just to get even with my husband!' she screamed. 'Screw you!'

She rolled up the window, floored the car and drove away, leaving BB staggering back to inspect the latest damage to his Cadillac just as Looney came walking out of the building, heading for his car.

Looney gazed at the smashed-up baby blue Cadillac and whistled.

'I think you ought to get rid of this car,' he said to BB. 'It's bad luck.'

As he spoke Nora's car could be heard screeching around the corner. Looney raised an eyebrow.

'Is that the guy again?'

'No, it's his wife,' BB said, trembling slightly.

Looney shook his head. 'There's some kind of sickness that runs in that family,' he said.

'"DAY-O! da, da, da; da, da, day . . . daylight come and he wanna go home . . ."'

Mouse was back on his banana boat.

'Why can't they get rid of that fucking record?' Tilley growled, turning from the table where he and Gil were playing pool to scowl at Mouse who was standing next to his beloved jukebox.

'It's not a hit any more,' Tilley grumbled. 'Nobody cares about this song any more . . . it's history.'

'"DAY-O! da, da, da, da, day . . ."' sang Mouse.

'We can always smash the jukebox, or break in and steal the record,' Gil suggested.

Tilley once again stooped to line up a shot. 'He's getting on my nerves,' he muttered. 'The guy eats like an animal, and sings like an asshole.'

'Maybe it's me,' Gil said guiltily, 'but I'm beginning to like it.'

Tilley aimed carefully and hit the ball, sinking the shot. 'Yes, sir . . . yes, sir!' he said happily. He still had the touch.

'Take a look at this crap,' said Sam, who had walked

through to the pool hall from the back office and now dropped an open envelope on the pool table in front of them.

'IRS?' Tilley groaned. 'They're not gonna leave me alone!'

'Home Improvement Commission,' Sam corrected him sourly.

A hush fell over all the tin men in the pool hall and even Mouse stopped singing. Tilley pulled out the letter and read it.

'We've got to appear?' he said anxiously.

Sam nodded. 'I think that's the gist of what they're saying.'

Gil, Mouse and a few other tin men gathered round the pool table and peered over Tilley's shoulder to read the letter.

'Holy Christ!' said Mouse.

'Can't we just ignore it?' Tilley suggested. 'How do they know we got the letter?'

'It's certified,' said Sam who knew what that meant from personal experience.

'What do you think, Sam?' said Tilley.

'I dunno ... I don't know what they've got.'

Tilley knew what they'd got. They'd got a big grudge against him personally.

'Why is this happening?' he wailed. 'Am I paranoid or something? I mean, why is this happening?' He turned to the other tin men as though they were in on the whole conspiracy.

'The government is after me ... the state is after me ... Mr Marengay ... somebody is always after me. What the hell's going on here? I'm just this guy. What's the big deal? They can't get along without me? The government can't operate unless they've got Tilley's money ... the Commission's after my job! This shit's driving me insane! All the lying, thieving, stealing corporations in the world, and the IRS takes the time to come for me? there's billions of dollars out there but they've got to come and get Tilley's four thousand dollars!'

The other tin men were staring at him in a strange way as though they were a party to the whole vendetta.

'What are you all staring at?' he growled, and then turned on Mouse. 'Turn off the fucking Belafonte song *now*, or I'm gonna break the goddamn machine!'

A night out with Stanley was about as much fun for BB as a day in church. They had ended up in the Corral Club bar where he was quickly getting drunk.

'Come on, Beeb, let's dance,' said one of the regular girls, as he sat drinking Scotch and beer and putting up with Stanley's ceaseless questions.

'Not tonight, Ruthie,' he replied blearily, 'my dancing shoes are on holiday.'

She looked very disappinted. Everyone knew BB was the best dancer in the club. 'You sure?'

He gave her a befuddled grin and slowly nodded. 'I'm more than sure.'

She walked off and he took another shot of whiskey, chasing it down with some more beer.

'Who was the best you ever saw?' Stanley asked eagerly.

BB opened an eye. 'Best I ever saw? Best tin man I ever saw?'

He held up his shot glass towards the bartender who instantly filled it up.

'Harry Apel... Dandy Flynn,' he began woozily, 'those guys had good lines but they burned themselves out too fast. Best? Moe's the best... the best there ever was. If he's in the door, he's got a sale. The best closer ever.'

Stanley lapped it up. 'What's some of the hustles he used to pull?'

BB downed another shot of whiskey.

'Goddamn Nora,' he mumbled. 'Goddamn Nora! I'm trying to adjust... I'm putting up with things I never put up with in my life. I mean, give me a break woman... give me a break.'

Stanley nodded politely and tried to get back to the tin business. 'So, what are a couple of things you and Moe have done?'

BB gazed into his glass. 'It was getting to be real pleasant... figure that.' He smiled. 'More than pleasant.' Then he drunkenly wrinkled up his nose. 'To hell with her!'

'How come Moe's so good?' Stanley persisted. 'Why do you think, huh?'

BB seemed at last to be coming back to him. He slowly pondered the question and then nodded as though agreeing to Stanley's proposition.

'Great man, Moe,' he sighed. 'Great man.'

He held out his glass again to the bartender who obligingly refilled it.

'I don't know why they're so irrational,' he mumbled, downing more Scotch and beer. 'Chicks... I dunno. I think it's because air gets inside 'em.' He burped. 'She probably went back home... to her husband.' He looked at his watch. 'Eleven thirty... he wouldn't be home yet.'

He took out a ten dollar bill from his wallet. 'This ought to cover it, Stanley,' BB muttered, putting the bill down on the bar, slipping off the bar stool and lurching out of the club, leaving Stanley looking after him, disappointed.

Tilley was too drunk to drive so Sam drove him home in his maroon Cadillac.

'They got no right,' Tilley grumbled from the passenger seat. 'You know what I'm saying, Sam? They've got no right.'

He brought out a bottle of whiskey from his pocket and took a slug.

'They've got nothing concrete against us,' Sam pointed out calmly, 'because if it's just hearsay stuff, it's neither here nor there.'

Didn't make any difference to those guys, Tilley thought morosely. If they couldn't plant any evidence on you they'd fabricate it – they'd use any trick to rob a man of his dignity and his livelihood: break into his house, steal his wife, wreck his car . . .

'Where's my car?' he mumbled. 'What happened to my car?' He looked round in panic: this wasn't his car.

'It's better I drop you off,' Sam said quietly.

Then he remembered: this was Sam's car.

'Yeah, it's better,' he groaned.

Chapter Twenty-One

Tilley ran the cold faucet in the bathroom, leaned his head over the sink and let the water splash over his face and hair for several minutes as he attempted to sober up, during which time he nodded off to sleep . . . Suddenly he jerked awake and banged his head on the faucet. Grabbing it in pain, he slowly slid down the tiled wall to the floor.

Outside in the street a baby blue Cadillac zigzagged along the middle of the road and pulled up at angle in front of Tilley's house, its front wheel on the sidewalk. BB popped his drunken head out of the window and looked up and down the street.

'He ain't here,' he mumbled.

Awkwardly he clambered out of the car and stumbled around the street, looking for Nora's Chevy among all the parked cars until finally falling over some trash cans in front of Tilley's house.

The noise penetrated Tilley's dreams and groggily he jerked awake once more, struggling to his feet and stumbling through to the bedroom as more trash cans rolled over. He peered out of the window and through a befuddled haze began to make out a figure crawling around the garbage cans. Slowly it dawned on him that the figure was that of Mr Marengay.

'I knew I could smell a rat!' he cried triumphantly as if this confirmed that far from suffering from paranoia his enemy was only too real. 'The son of a bitch is coming for me . . . the son of a bitch never wants to leave me alone!'

The vision – real or imaginary – had at least had the positive effect of sobering Tilley up: he walked over to the night table, opened the drawer and pulled out a revolver.

As BB lurched his way up the front steps to Tilley's house, Tilley made his way out of the bedroom and down the stairs. Quietly he crept to the front door.

'You want to rob my goddamn house?' he muttered quietly. 'I'm gonna make it easy for you.' He unlocked the door, leaving it ajar. 'Come and rob Tilley,' he whispered, 'come on . . . take everything's he got.'

Outside, BB stood gazing giddily at the door, wondering what he was going to say to her. At last he plucked up the courage to knock on the door – which, with a little creak, swung open. Taken aback somewhat, he stood there for a few moments indecisively, then stepped inside.

'Hel –' he started to say.

But Tilley whipped around from behind the door and bashed him hard on the head with the butt of his gun and BB instantly slumped, unconscious, to the floor.

Tilley switched on the kitchen light and went over to a cupboard, taking out a large china bowl; then he opened the refrigerator and began putting eggs and rotten tomatoes into the bowl. He pulled out a piece of celery from the salad section, but it was soft and wilted, so he threw it away; he began to select other vegetables – potatoes, carrots, onions – but then changed his mind, deciding to settle for the eggs and tomatoes. He closed the refrigerator door and made his way to the living room where BB was now lying, still unconscious, on the floor. Cautiously Tilley sat down across the room from him with the bowl on his lap.

'You're a sick man!' he shouted. 'You smash my car, you steal my wife, and now you come to rob me! You're one demented human being.'

Slowly BB started to come to, groggily trying to work out where he was, why he was lying on a floor, who was shouting at him and what was hitting him.

What was hitting him was the egg that Tilley threw at him: it landed on his head.

'What're you doing?' BB mumbled, too dazed to move.

'What do ya want to break into my house for?' Tilley streamed back. 'This ain't the fucking Rockefeller Mansion! There ain't thirty-eight television sets here. They ain't saying, "Nelson, I think we've had a break-in... count the sets to see how many we've got left." There ain't tons of jewelry hanging out of drawers... it ain't like I don't know which watch to put on, I got so many. I'm a working man, trying to make an honest living. What fucking morality you got, asshole?'

He threw another egg at BB, again hitting him on the head. As egg yolk started to drop down his face, he gasped and grunted, trying to get off the floor, but too drunk and stunned from the effect of the blow to his head from Tilley's gun to manage it.

'You're the craziest human being on the face of this earth!' he groaned as Tilley got ready with another egg.

'What else do you want from me?' Tilley screamed. 'Huh? What else? I've got enough problems with the IRS busting my balls and the Home Improvement Commission bullshit to contend with. I don't need aggravation from you.'

'Nobody does this to me and lives!' BB spluttered as he wiped his face and tried once more to get up. 'Nobody!'

'How do ya like your eggs?' Tilley jeered and threw another one. 'Over easy?' He picked up a tomato. 'Side of tomatoes?' He hurled it at BB's face.

'You're going to rue the day you ran into my car,' BB groaned. 'This ain't the end . . . this is just the beginning.'

In reply, Tilley threw another egg.

Tilley couldn't believe it. The guy had broken into his house and he was being charged with assault.

'A guy breaks into my house and I'm being charged with assault?' he said indignantly to the police officer down at police headquarters. 'It makes no sense.'

'Let's get it down right,' said Police Sergeant Calloway, bringing out a pencil and notebook. 'The guy broke into your house, you hit him in the head with a gun, went to the refrigerator, took out eggs and tomatoes and threw them at him.'

'I was defending myself,' Tilley protested. 'He was stealing from me.'

'It doesn't sound like defense to me,' Calloway remarked.

'I wanted to humiliate the guy. Here I am, out busting my ass all day making a decent living, I come home, and some schmuck is trying to steal from me.'

Calloway nodded. 'So you hit him with a gun, and pelted him with eggs and tomatoes?'

Tilley knew his rights. 'If I had some soup I would have thrown soup at him . . . is there any law you can't throw eggs?'

Calloway put down his pencil and eyed Tilley. 'Mr Babowski claims he didn't break into your house.'

'What did I do?' Tilley growled. 'Invite him in so that I could throw eggs at him?'

'Maybe Mr Babowski intended to break into your house,' Callowy conceded, 'but these circumstances of the guy being pelted with eggs and tomatoes is something we need to look into.'

Tilley shrugged. 'He's lucky that he didn't rob me last

week, 'cos then my wife was living at home and we had all kinds of things in the fridge... I could have thrown barley soup, pumpkin pie, candied yams... yeah, he got off light.'

Chapter Twenty-Two

'I can't believe it,' BB said to Bagel as they left the police station. 'The man throws eggs at me and now I'm gonna have breakfast with him.'

He still had egg stains all over his suit, and a purple bruise on his forehead but fortunately the blow Tilley had delivered with the gun butt had not been very heavy – BB's slump into unconsciousness could mainly be put down to the booze he'd drunk the previous evening.

Even so, the idea of having breakfast with this maniac was already making his stomach churn. Who knows, he might start throwing eggs at him again.

As far as Bagel was concerned the sooner BB sorted out this thing the better. With Moe in hospital and BB in his present state, how could he run a business?

'His partner says maybe the two of you can sit down and come to some kind of settlement,' he reminded BB.

'What am I supposed to say to him?' Tilley was grumbling to Sam as they sat in Tilley's car. 'The man has been a pain in the ass since the day he rammed into my car.'

'Just air your differences and we'll put an end to this,' Sam advised him.

The two Cadillacs pulled out of the police station parking lot and headed for the coffee shop.

Although BB and Tilley did not actually speak to each other for the first five minutes no one threw any eggs and

Sam and Bagel held the conversation together between intervals when the four men studiously examined their menus.

Finally it was BB who came to the point.

'I tell you what,' he said, looking up from his menu and straight at Tilley, 'I'll drop the charges against you, and we can wipe the slate clean.'

Tilley stared at him, thrown completely off-balance. 'I appreciate it,' he said gruffly.

Sam and Bagel smiled with relief.

'See how quickly you can clear it up,' Sam said.

Unfortunately, Tilley hadn't quite finished.

'But I don't understand how the slate gets wiped clean when he breaks into my house and I'm the one charged,' he went on, his voice rising with every syllable.

BB glowered at him. 'I told you, I wasn't breaking into your house. I was looking for your wife.'

Tilley held up his hand. 'All right . . . all right,' he said calmly, secretly gratified to have provoked the son of a bitch into losing his cool. 'I'm too tired . . . the slate's clean . . . the slate's clean.'

'What will you have?' said the waitress.

'Couple of eggs over,' Tilley launched in, 'some hash browns, some toast – toasted dark . . . butter on the side, large grapefruit juice and some coffee.'

She was busily writing the order when Tilley changed his mind.

'On second thought,' he snapped, 'instead of the eggs over, if I ordered soft boiled eggs do you take them out of the shell or leave them in the shells?'

Sam, who was used to this, merely rolled his eyes, but BB was finding it hard to contain his intense irritation.

'We leave them in the shell,' the waitress replied wearily.

Tilley pulled a face. 'I don't like them that way because they get hot in the hand and it's hard to scoop the stuff out . . . it's not good . . . and you get little bits of shell in there and it doesn't taste good.'

'Why don't you just order some scrambled eggs and be done with it,' BB growled. 'All right?'

Tilley shook his head. 'If I'm going to order, at least I ought to be content with my food.'

'I'm getting a little hungry,' BB snapped, doing his best to keep his cool. 'I've got a headache as it is. Just order some eggs so some other people can have something to eat before the lunch trade comes in.'

Tilley appealed to Sam. 'Why do I need a guy telling me what I should or shouldn't eat?'

BB gritted his teeth. 'This is not a four-star restaurant . . . we're not having a gourmet meal . . . we're ordering breakfast for Christ's sake!'

Tilley was having a ball. 'It so happens I haven't been to this restaurant before. I don't know how they do their eggs . . . if they've over easy and they're gooey, I'm not happy with it . . . and I'm not happy if the soft-boiled eggs are left in the shell–'

'Can I have some French toast and a cup of coffee?' BB cut him off, turning to the waitress. 'Bagel, what do you want?'

'Hey! I'm ordering here,' Tilley said angrily. 'At least you can have the courtesy to let a man order his breakfast.' He turned to Sam as if BB wasn't sitting with them. 'Sam, this guy gets on my nerves . . . from day one! I knew it then and I know it now.'

He stood up from the table and started to leave.

'I'm back pressing charges against you!' BB shouted at him.

Tilley swung round so that he was directly facing his enemy. 'You want to play that way?' he shouted back. 'This game ain't over . . . mister . . . it ain't over . . .'

He turned and stormed out.

Sam stood up, shrugged apologetically and followed

his partner.

As far as BB was concerned he was the outright winner of this little game. He'd done his best, he'd kept his cool. The guy had shown himself up for what he was: an asshole.

'So, I'm having French toast and coffee,' he said calmly to the waitress. 'Bagel?'

Chapter Twenty-Three

It looked like Moe was going to pull through. The heart operation had been a success but it was going to be a long time before BB would be working with his partner again.

It was strange seeing him lying there hooked up to all those tubes like he was now dependent on them to stay alive when Moe had always struck BB as the kind of guy who'd tried not to depend on anyone – except May of course.

'Moe, when you decided to marry May, how did you know?' BB asked him as he sat by his bedside.

'Know what?' His breathing was still difficult and BB had been warned not to tire him.

'How did ya know?'

'You mean to make up my mind to marry her?' said Moe.

'Yeah. How did ya know?'

Moe shrugged.

'This Nora is a pain in the ass, Moe . . . a pain in the ass,' BB said angrily. 'It's worse now than when she used to be around.'

Moe smiled.

'You wanna hear something. The other night at the Coral Club, I turned down a dance.'

'You turned down a dance?' Moe looked astonished.

'What's the odds on that? You think you can come up with odds on that one?'

'Hundred to one BB don't dance,' Moe rapped out

instantly. 'A hundred to one against.'

They sat in silence for a while but BB had the feeling that Moe had something particular to say to him. When he finally came out with it, it was – literally – hard for him to do so and, as BB might have guessed, it was about the tin game.

'I'm getting out of the business, BB . . .' he wheezed. 'I've got nothing for all this.'

'Lot of good times, Moe,' BB reminded him.

'A lot of good times,' Moe agreed, 'but I can't live off the good times . . . You know, my brother-in-law has offered me a job at Hess Shoes. I think maybe I should do it. You get there in the morning, you come home at night . . . you get health benefits . . . I get to be assistant manager.'

BB didn't know what to say so he said what he felt. 'That's it, Moe? You're gonna spend the day measuring people's feet? "You're an 'E' fit . . . you're a 'D' wide . . . you got a high arch . . . I'll show you something in an alligator . . . something with a wing tip . . ." How can you talk about that all day long?'

Moe didn't answer.

'Moe, you're the best tin man there ever was,' BB said from the heart. 'Nobody's a better closer.'

'It's over, BB,' Moe said quietly. 'It's over.'

BB gazed at his old partner. A lump rose in his throat and he felt a slight shiver.

'So, May's happy about this Hess Shoe thing, heh?' he said a little hoarsely.

Moe grinned. 'To say the least.'

'You know, when I saw *Bonanza* the other day, something occurred to me,' Sam remarked to Tilley as he drove along in his Cadillac. 'There's those three guys living on the Ponderosa and you never hear them say anything about wanting to get laid. You never hear Hoss turn to Little Joe and say, "I had such a hard-on when I woke up this morning." You know... they never talk about broads... nothing. Ya never hear Little Joe say, "Hey, Hoss, I went into Virginia City and saw a girl with the greatest ass I ever saw in my life." Ya just see 'em walking around the Ponderosa saying, "Yes, Pa," and "Where's Little Joe?" Nothing about broads.

'I don't think I'm being too picky... at least once if they talked about getting horny. I don't care if you're living on the Ponderosa or right here in Baltimore, guys talk about getting laid.'

He sighed sadly. 'I'm beginning to think that show doesn't have realism. What do you think, Tilley?'

'Sam, I can't concentrate on *Bonanza* shit,' Tilley snapped. 'I've got too much on my brain, what with that asshole and the Home Improvement Commission. I don't want to have to worry about whether Little Joe got laid last night.'

Sam looked a little grazed – not wounded, just grazed, but when Tilley suggested they had a bite to eat he lightened up.

'Yeah,' he said cheerfully, 'we'll go and have some lunch at the Smorgasbord.'

Tilley stared at all the salads, just as Sam had described them – laid out all over the place like a miniature farm – and started to wonder. Maybe Sam had a point after all. Maybe God was right here in Thor's Smorgasbord Restaurant, sprouting out of the cauliflowers and lettuce. Why not? After all, if he were God he'd much rather come here than go to church to let people know he was around.

Sam had already filled up his tray at the buffet and moved off to the cashier but Tilley hung behind, gazing at God in all his many forms and expressions. Then he lifted his eyes to the ceiling.

'God,' he murmured, 'if you're responsible for all the stuff down here, maybe you got a moment's attention for me... Between the IRS, this Home Improvement Commission and Mr Marengay, I got it up to here with this bullshit. To be frank with you, I'm in the toilet here. If you can see your way —'

He was interrupted by a woman with a tray who was attempting to reach over him.

'Listen,' he snapped at her, 'I'm praying here... go around.'

'I wanted to get some of the salad,' she said indignantly.

'It's out of order... go around.'

He waved her past him like a traffic cop. She stared at him angrily but moved down the line.

'Do what you can, all right?' he finished hastily. 'I appreciate it. Amen.'

He quickly helped himself to a variety of God's many bounties.

Chapter Twenty-Four

It had been a week now since Nora had tried to drive BB down in her Chevy. He had held off trying to get in touch with her for as long as he could. He couldn't blame her for being mad at him but, he decided, she would by now have cooled off and be prepared to listen to his explanation. Maybe she was even missing him like he was missing her.

He had dialled the number three times already that morning and each time put the phone down when the switchboard lady answered. This time he'd go through with it.

He picked up the phone again and dialled.

'Nora Tilley, please,' he said nervously.

'What department is she with?' came a woman's voice.

'She's with social security.'

'Which department in social security?'

He hadn't considered this. 'I dunno,' he said, racking his brains. She was just a secretary, that's all he knew. 'She's there somewhere . . . yeah, on the third floor . . . she's got a desk towards the back.'

'Just a moment . . . checking.'

Behind him, Stanley was stooping over a filing cabinet looking through the files.

Cheese noticed this and wandered over to him.

'Stanley, can I help you with something?'

'No,' he replied casually, 'I'm just making myself busy.'

'Well, I wouldn't do that,' Cheese advised him. 'Bagel doesn't like nobody looking at the files.'

BB was starting to wonder whether Nora might have packed in her job as well as her husband, but then her voice came on the line.

'Mrs Tilley,' she said. No one ever rang her at work.

'Nora,' he said excitedly, 'this is BB.'

The phone instantly went dead. BB stared at it for a moment and then reluctantly put the receiver down.

So far they'd managed to run rings round the Commission and Tilley was feeling very pleased with himself. Could it be that God had got the message in the smorgasbord restaurant?

Masters leaned into the microphone to continue his interrogation of Tilley and Sam.

'Didn't you approach Mr Boloshevski August 18, 1961, while he was cutting his front lawn and tell him that his house had been selected, as one of only sixteen homes in the State of Maryland, for a free aluminum siding job?'

'What's the name again?' said Tilley.

Masters sighed. These guys were getting to be so predictable. 'Boloshevski,' he repeated.

Tilley appeared to be thinking hard. Finally he shrugged. 'Doesn't ring a bell . . . Sam, does it ring a bell to you?'

Sam leaned into the microphone. 'It doesn't ring a bell to me either, sir,' he replied vacantly.

'Didn't you suggest,' Masters persevered, 'that for a nominal labor charge, he would receive over five thousand dollars worth of aluminum siding?'

'That's an awful lot for nothing,' Tilley replied. 'Doesn't sound like good business to me.'

'Mr Boloshevski was ultimately charged twenty-four hundred dollars for labor, which according to our figures is about the average cost of an aluminum siding job.'

Sam looked bewildered. 'I don't get the point of this.'

Masters patiently spelt it out. 'Twenty-four hundred dollars that you charged for labor is the same as if Mr Boloshevski had purchased the aluminum siding and had the labor done.'

'Maybe I'm missing the point here,' Tilley put in, 'but if he paid twenty-four hundred, which is the cost of the job, I can't see anything wrong with that. I don't know the guy but I don't quite get the problem.'

Masters cleared his throat. 'What we're getting at here... what we're trying to stress, is that the job was sold under false terms. The man didn't win any award... he was not getting aluminum siding at a special price. A clear case of deception was involved here.'

Tilley really couldn't see what point Masters was making. 'What's he talking about?' he whispered to Sam. 'The man got the job for twenty-four hundred dollars and that's what it costs in aluminum siding.'

'Uh...' he leaned into the microphone, 'I don't know... we have no recollection of this particular job, but I don't know if this is deception. Look, if you work in a clothing store, some guy tries on a suit, it looks like shit, but you tell him it looks wonderful. The guy's standing there looking like a sack of shit, the salesman says what a great suit and the man buys it. That's deception as far as I can see, but I don't understand the deceptiveness that you say we're responsible for... if I make myself clear.'

'I'd go along with that as well,' said Sam.

Masters took a deep breath. 'What we're trying to establish,' he said wearily, 'are the principles that have been laid down as part of the Home Improvement code of ethics... that you cannot mislead someone intentionally, and I think that's the principle that applies to this.'

'Did somebody put a gun to this guy's head and make

him spend twenty-four hundred dollars?' Tilley asked indignantly. 'I don't get the point here. I don't know the specifics of this case, not being privy to all the information, but all I can say is this guy got a fair price for a fair job.'

There was a hurried consultation between Masters and the five other Commissioners at the table, then another Commissioner, Bud Delaney, took the microphone to interrogate Tilley.

'Do you know Mr and Mrs Rayburn of 156 Aberdeen Avenue, Essex?'

Tilley glanced at Sam and shrugged his shoulders. 'I think you'd have to familiarise me,' he said into the microphone.

Delaney referred to a sheaf of papers in front of him. 'The couple purchased twenty-eight hundred dollars worth of aluminum siding and the two of you were the salesmen on record. They say, and I quote here —' he put on his spectacles and picked up a paper '— "that they would have received one hundred and fifty dollars per home for every person in the neighborhood who saw their house and decided to buy aluminum siding".' He looked up from the paper, removing his spectacles and peered at Tilley. 'Is that true?'

'It sounds right,' Tilley replied noncommittally.

'Are you aware that, according to the Home Improvement code, you are not allowed to exceed a twenty dollar limit in incentives?'

Tilley shrugged. 'We wanted to be a little more generous, that's all.'

'The couple said that they never did receive any money from any other jobs, as you had promised,' Delaney pointed out.

'We didn't get any leads from them,' Sam replied simply. 'Their house was not the show place that we thought it would be. It didn't generate the activity that we had hoped.'

'But should a referral turn up in the community,' Tilley chipped in, 'we'd be more than happy to give them twenty dollars instead of the hundred and fifty.'

Delaney stared at Tilley; then Masters leaned across the table and whispered to him.

'Excuse us for one moment,' Masters said into the microphone.

Tilley and Sam watched as Masters and Delaney conferred; then Masters leaned across to the other Commissioners, holding his hand over the microphone. Eventually they nodded in approval and Masters spoke once more into the microphone.

'Thank you very much, gentlemen,' he announced. 'Should there be a reason in the future to call you back, we would like to reserve that right.'

'Glad we could be of some service,' Tilley said from the Defense table.

Then he and Sam got up from the table and walked out of the building.

'We beat 'em, Sam!' he said gleefully, rubbing his hands, as they made their way to his car. 'We beat 'em! What a piece of cake! No problem! They ain't got nothing on us . . . clean as a whistle . . . we're clean as a whistle!'

Sam was, to say the least, feeling less jubilant. 'I need a drink,' he said dolefully. 'I hate inquisitions.'

Chapter Twenty-Five

It was raining heavily when Nora left the Social Security office and as she walked quickly across to the parking lot she held her umbrella tightly above her. So it should have been a complete surprise to her when BB suddenly slipped under the umbrella with her. But maybe she was expecting it, because her reaction was sharp and instant.

'I don't want to see you any more,' she said coldly, pulling away from him and continuing to walk towards her Chevy.

'I gotta talk to you,' BB shouted out behind her as the rain soaked through his jacket and shirt.

'I don't want to listen,' she snapped.

'Give me a chance to explain,' he begged. 'You owe me that much.'

'I don't owe you anything,' Nora said without turning.

BB let her walk away. Maybe it was for the best, he thought. She didn't need a guy like him. What kind of life could he offer her? A tin man didn't keep regular hours. He was never at home most of the time and then he might be home for a week on end and they'd get on each other's nerves...

Seems better than if she wasn't there, he heard Moe saying. At the time it had sounded like one of those negative responses you got from the customer when you couldn't close the deal and you knew it was really because they were attached to their old house with all its lousy wooden paneling and you'd never get them to change their mind because it came from somewhere deep in their life. He'd never felt like that about anything in his life – except maybe selling tin – until this moment. But now he realised he didn't care that much about the tin game any more. It was like Moe said, *It's over*. He thought of Tilley being a wise-ass in the coffee shop – he'd seen those kind of cheap tricks all through his life and he was up to here with them.

Seems better than if she wasn't there . . .

In the distance he could see that Nora had nearly reached her Chevy and he began to run towards her.

'It was a lousy thing to do, okay?' he shouted out. 'It was a lousy thing to use you to get back at your husband . . . but the fact is that I never would have met you otherwise!'

She was only yards away from her car when she stopped and turned to look at him.

'It was lousy,' he said as they finally stood face to face in the rain. 'It was a disgusting, terrible thing . . . but a lot of good came out of it.'

'What kind of a person would come up with such a devious thing?' she said slowly, almost like she was a little girl trying to understand why there had to be such a thing as evil in the world.

He suddenly realised how much he'd hurt her. Not even Tilley, he guessed, could have done a thing like that, but then it wasn't Tilley's style. Tilley's style was more . . . well, the guy probably just drove her crazy.

'I'm not always a nice guy, I admit that,' he said, looking into her eyes. 'I got a lot of training in deceit . . . it's an occupational hazard.'

He tried to laugh, but it didn't seem very funny.

'I'd like to know what it is about me that I have to fall for tin men,' she said, half to herself, though her eyes remained transfixed by his. 'What kind of character flaw do I have?'

'I didn't want to have to come here,' said BB who also seemed to be talking from somewhere within himself – not like she wasn't there: more like they were inside each other.

'I wish that I didn't have to ever see you again,' he said angrily. 'I've gone this far in my life without having to have this kind of thing happen to me. I was going through life, sailing along, pretty good ... doing okay, and I tried to get even with some crazy guy ... and I'm here.'

'The wet becomes you,' she said softly. 'Gets rid of some of the slickness.'

BB seemed to be wrestling with himself. 'I don't like the idea that I'm not in control of this, but if this stuff's got to happen, I guess I've got no choice. I wanna ... ya know ...'

He stared at her, getting angry.

'I wanna be with ya!' he shouted. 'Okay, I said that ... I said it, okay? I wanna be with ya! It pisses the hell out of me, and I'm gonna tell you that to your face, but I want to be with you ... I'd like to live with you because ... I miss you and I'd like to live with you ... I'd like to marry you ... and that's that!'

Nora eyed BB carefully as the rain fell on her umbrella and beat on his head.

Finally she sighed. 'I was hoping for something a little more romantic ... but, okay.'

It was like she'd granted him his life.

The flicker of a smile came into his face.

Sam had been working up to telling Tilley for – what was it? – days, weeks, months ... but somehow the place and time hadn't been quite right. But now as they sat at the bar of the Pimlico Hotel, nursing a couple of drinks, he got around to the subject. A pianist was playing 'Last

Night When We Were Young' and a few people were sitting around the piano joining in with the song. They were both pleasantly relaxed – even Tilley – and they'd been reminiscing on the old days before they'd worked together as partners.

'Ya know, Tilley,' he said lightly, 'we been working together for over a year.'

'Yeah, must be about that.'

Sam hesitated, quickly glanced at him, then took the plunge. 'I've been thinking that sometimes a different combination makes for better luck. Ya know what I mean? I mean, maybe the two of us ain't the right combination.'

Tilley stared at him in surprise. 'I'm just getting used to ya, Sam,' he pointed out.

'Let's face it,' Sam sighed, 'we're not exactly setting the world on fire.'

'It's a slump,' Tilley said gloomily, 'it's a slump, Sam.'

He nodded, determined that Tilley should get the message. 'Maybe it's a slump, but like baseball, some time they have to change the lineup to get the team going again.'

Tilly frowned and Sam felt like a heel.

'You're not serious about this, are you Sam?' he said slowly.

'Yeah,' Sam muttered.

'You're serious? You wanna get another partner? You don't think I'm gonna pull out of this?'

Et tu, Brute, Tilley thought despondently.

'I know you're gonna . . . I know you're gonna,' Sam said wretchedly.

'So?'

Sam drank up his Scotch and turned to face his partner. 'Look,' he said earnestly, 'we beat the Commission today . . . you know, we got a little bit of a victory. We split right now and maybe we can add to that . . . you know what I'm saying?'

Tilley had got the message loud and clear. 'I know . . . I know,' he said in a tone of resignation. 'Change in the lineup. Okay, maybe it'll help . . . maybe it'll help.' He drank his whiskey quickly. 'You got any ideas for a new partner?'

'Well, I had a conversation with Solly Shavitz, so . . . maybe I'll go with him.'

He sneaked a look at Tilley: he seemed to be taking it very well which only made Sam feel more guilty.

'Mouse is gonna need a new partner because Dennis is going into used cars,' he suggested.

Tilley scowled. 'Mouse! Mouse!' He gets on my nerves . . . He eats too much.'

He sighed and held up his whiskey glass. 'Here's to some pretty good times, huh?'

Sam grinned, relieved, and joined in the toast.

Chapter Twenty-Six

Looney was back from Florida, looking tanned and relaxed, though still twitching and blinking. A lot seemed to have been going on in his absence: for one thing there was BB and Nora.

'I don't get it,' he said to Stanley as they sat at the Corral Club bar watching BB dancing intimately with his enemy's wife. 'The broad smashes into his car and he takes her dancing. Some kind of dating ritual that I'm not familiar with.'

Stanley nodded. 'BB's a pretty good tin man, huh?' he started to pump.

'Pretty good? Whew!' Looney whistled. 'Man's what legends are made of. Started selling pots and pans door to door at sixteen. Nothing he can't sell . . .

The song ended and BB walked Nora back to the table they were sitting at. He didn't remember when he'd felt so good.

'You're gonna come back and stay the night?' he asked her.

She hesitated. 'I dunno . . . all my things are back at Nellie's – the other side of town.' She thought for a moment. 'I know what I could do, I'll go back home – I mean, to Tilley's house,' she corrected herself. 'There's still a few things I left behind . . . at least I can get a change of clothes.'

They sat down and he looked at her. 'I'm glad this is working out.'

She studied his face. 'You really happy?'

'Yeah,' he said truthfully.

Nora frowned. 'You don't really show a great deal of exuberance.'

'Honey,' BB said, 'for me . . . I'm a parade.'

He should have expected it. They were putting the screws on him, all of them – first it had just been Nora, then Marengay stepped onto the scene, then the Commission got in on the act, and that evening Sam had joined the party. Now the IRS had locked him out of his house and slapped a new padlock on the door. With his luck, he thought as he stood at his front door trying to break open the padlock, some friendly neighbor would call the cops and the courts would eat him up. He'd be given the electric chair for trying to get into his own home.

Behind him a car pulled up and he heard familiar footsteps.

'What happened?' Nora said, standing at the bottom of the front steps.

He shrugged. 'The IRS . . . they need my furniture. They got some living room somewhere in this country that needs to be furnished.'

'They're taking the furniture?' she said, without too much surprise.

'The furniture, the whole house,' he muttered angrily. 'They locked it up . . . they confiscated it.'

'What do you expect?' she yelled up to him on the porch. 'You expect to get some preferential treatment . . . you're some special case? You've got to pay your taxes just like everybody else has to pay their taxes!'

She seemed to have pressed a cut-out switch in him. He shrugged the way he had all through their marriage.

'How many arguments did we used to have about filing your taxes?' she said, calming down a little. After all, it wasn't her problem any longer.

'We had a lot of arguments,' he said wearily.

She walked up the steps and sat down next to him on the porch. 'There's a responsibility that you've got to have,' she said quietly. 'It's a long way from high school, Tilley.'

He sighed, trying to make sense of it all. 'I was doing pretty good there for a while . . . doing pretty good. Had my house, had a wife, a Cadillac . . . I still got my Cadillac,' he consoled himself.

She gazed at him. There were bags under his eyes. He looked a wreck.

'Where are you gonna sleep?' she asked.

'I'll stay at Sam's for a couple of days until I get set up.' He glanced at her curiously. 'What're you doing here, anyway?'

'There's just a couple of things you didn't throw out of the house . . . a couple of things I didn't find on the lawn. I assume they're still in the drawer.'

Tilley shrugged. 'I don't know . . . I did a pretty good house cleaning number on you.'

'Listen,' she changed the subject, 'about the divorce. Do you want to file, or should I file?'

'I got to be frank with you,' he scowled, 'this guy is nuts.'

'He told me all about it . . . all about how you threw eggs at him.'

'He told you it was about eggs?' Tilley said angrily, suddenly seeming to come to life. 'The guy tried to break into my house. He tried to steal things from me.'

'He was trying to find me,' Nora reminded him. 'We had an argument.'

'I think you'd be making a big mistake if you married him,' he insisted.

Nora was getting angry again. 'It's not for you to make decisions for me.'

'I think maybe I should, because I think you're being misled . . . I think you're confused. I think —'

'I know what I'm doing,' she interrupted him.

'Nora, listen to me,' he said passionately. 'I know about guys —'

'I appreciate your concern,' she cut him off coldly, 'but it's not for you to tell —'

'But this guy is as bad a choice as you could make. Bad choice.'

Nora could feel herself being wound up. It was something Tilley did. Maybe he didn't mean to do it but it was something he did. 'You're a good one to give advice,' she said, breathing hard, 'you're sitting on the steps, locked out of your house because you can't pay your taxes, and you're going to give me advice on life?'

Tilley had miraculously calmed down. 'I'm not giving you a divorce, and that's it. I'm looking out for your welfare. No divorce.'

About to respond, she looked at him and realised it was pointless. Instead she stood up and walked down the steps towards her car.

'It's for your own benefit,' he yelled after her, 'and you'll thank me for it.'

She turned back to face him and suddenly exploded with all the anger that had been building up inside her.

'*My* benefit!' she screamed. 'You don't give a damn about me! You don't give a damn who I marry. The reason you don't want me to marry him is because he's the one taking your wife, and you've got your own problems with him. You don't care about me . . . it's your same bullshit your doing. That's what it always is with you, Tilley. It's always you! The IRS took *your* house . . . *your* furniture! You don't say anything about my things in the house. I've got things in the house I worked damn hard for, and things that belonged to my family . . . the headboard that was given to me by Aunt Josephine, it's got to be at least a hundred years old. You don't care if they take it away. It's all you, Tilley! That's what it's always been.'

She stood there for a moment longer, then turned back to her car, climbed in, slammed and drove away, leaving Tilley still standing on the front steps.

'Women,' he sighed to himself. 'Too emotional . . . too emotional.'

Chapter Twenty-Seven

'Thanks for the lift back, BB,' Stanley said, as the baby blue Cadillac drew up outside the Superior Aluminum building. 'See ya around,'

BB glanced up at the building: it looked oddly unreal at this time of the night, like an old warehouse in a gangster movie, like a part of his past.

'Okay, Stanley,' he said.

The young man got out of the car and watched as BB turned the corner and drove off, then he walked quickly towards the office door.

Stanley was feeling rather pleased with himself. It was easy enough to get the salesman to talk: just buy them a few drinks and they'd talk all night, expecting you to believe that there was something admirable, even legendary, about these sordid hustlers and their fraudulent tricks. The trouble was that none of it would stand up at the Hearings – it was all hearsay and what he'd needed was a few names and dates which he could check with the files.

Which was why this evening had been highly productive. Looney's vacation in Florida had loosened his tongue to such an extent that Stanley had been able to memorise a whole list of clients who had been deceived by Superior salesman, but particularly by Gable and Babowski who seemed to be the arch-practitioners of every example of unscrupulous sales malpractice that the

Commission had on its books – plus a whole lot more that they had personally originated.

It had taken him less than fifteen minutes to locate the relevant customer files and cross refer them to files organised by sales staff. At last he had everything he needed. He turned to leave – and jumped with alarm.

'You know something, Stanley, I can always smell a guy who's not made of tin.'

BB walked towards him from the doorway. 'It's against the law to steal files. I could call and have you arrested and sent to jail, right now.'

Stanley seemed to go through several contortions until settling for a placatory gesture.

'I'll put everything back,' he smirked sheepishly, 'nobody's the wiser.'

'You work for the Commission, is that it?' BB snapped.

Stanley nodded reluctantly.

'Doesn't the Commission have enough information? They got to send out guys like you to spy?'

Stanley adopted a confidential tone. 'Well, we just started out,' he explained, 'and if we had some really good hard facts of some infractions, it would give us a lot of credibility in the community.'

BB walked towards Stanley, looked at him sourly and then grabbed him by his tie, pushing him backwards until Stanley crashed into the filing cabinet.

'You know what your big problem is, Stanley?' BB snarled. 'You're lazy. If you want to find out stuff, then you dig... you get on the phone... you canvas... "We're from the Home Improvement Commission..." Go find the leads... that's what we do all the time. You're just lazy, Stanley. If we're doing something wrong, you should collect all your evidence. Instead, you snoop around... steal files.'

He looked around the office, shaking his head. 'What

is this? Undercover time? You think you're breaking up some big drug ring? Is this the Mafia you've infiltrated? All you've got here is a bunch of guys selling tin for Christ sake!'

He glanced at the files Stanley had been about to steal, recognising several customers whom he and Moe had signed up, others who were just down to Moe's solo efforts. He slammed the files down on the desk.

'You want some files?' he spat, then walked over to the filing cabinet, flipped through some files and pulled out several, throwing them down on the desk.

'Here . . . here's some jobs I did,' he shouted as Stanley got up from the floor. 'Leave Moe out of this . . . he quit the business.'

Awkwardly, hastily, Stanley gathered up the files from the desk.

'Go on,' BB shouted, 'get out of here.'

Stanley started for the door, then hesitated, and turned back.

'Why are you doing this?' he said pale-faced.

'If it's not gonna be you, it's gonna be somebody else,' BB muttered, 'and if it's not tonight, it's gonna be another time.'

Stanley still looked puzzled, but made a hasty exit, leaving BB to pick up the files he had been attempting to steal and return them to the cabinet. Then he shut the cabinet drawer with a harsh slam.

Nora told him about Tilley that night after they had made love. Having sex with Nora after the incident with Stanley and before hearing about Tilley was like caviar stuck between two stale slices of bread.

'Maybe if I talked to him another day he'll change his mind,' she said. 'I mean, he's like that . . . one day he's this way and another day he's that way.'

BB didn't want to hear about the asshole. 'You don't

need to talk to him,' he said.

'I mean,' Nora went on 'he's probably, you know, upset about the IRS taking the house and all our stuff.'

'Ever see a Volkswagen,' he said casually.

'What?'

'You know,' he said, drawing a little diagram with his finger on her shoulder, 'those little Volkswagens.'

Nora didn't. 'What does that mean?' she said examining her shoulder.

BB sighed, amused. 'It's a car . . . a little car.'

She stared at him, baffled. 'What does that have to do with anything?'

'I dunno,' he said vaguely, 'they're interesting.'

Tin men, Nora thought, she'd never figure them out however many she lived with.

Chapter Twenty-Eight

Tilley stood back and considered the new wording as Wing chalked out the schedules and sales on the blackboard.

'Tilley and Mouse,' he repeated. 'It looks weird, doesn't it? Looks very weird.'

'Let's hope you have some better luck with Mouse,' Wing said drily.

'Hey, Tilley,' Gil called out from the pool hall, 'Mr Marengay's out here.'

'Can I talk to you in private,' said BB as Tilley came out of the office, 'or do I have to talk to you over fourteen pool tables?'

Tilley moved down the pool hall towards him.

'We've got enough that's going down between the two of us,' BB went on, 'but the fact of the matter is that I love your wife and I want to marry her.'

Tilley grinned. Then he laughed in BB's face. 'I don't care who she marries, but I don't want her marrying you!'

Why does the guy have to turn everything into a personal contest? BB thought. 'Why don't we just talk about this in a nice rational manner,' he said, trying to stay calm.

'Rational?' Tilley sneered. 'You're going to be rational?'

'We've got our problems, but let's try and isolate this particular situation.'

Tilley screwed up his eyes and did a double take.

'Isolate . . . isolate?' he jeered. 'I like this kind of talk. What the hell nonsense is that?'

BB tried to keep a grip on himself. 'What are you gonna gain from this thing here?'

'Now let me see here,' Tilley mocked him. 'I've got to *isolate* that for a moment and think it over.'

'Nobody's going to benefit from making me mad,' said BB, breathing hard.

'You ought to hear yourself,' Tilley taunted him. 'You know that? You ought to listen to the way you talk. You come in here, you want to take my wife . . . you want to isolate the situation . . . you want to be rational.' He shook his head scornfully. 'I've got no tolerance for you, mister. You know what I'm saying?'

BB had had enough. 'What you're saying is you don't want to discuss this, am I right?'

Tilley neatly shifted gear. 'You like pool?'

What was the little jerk up to now? BB wondered.

'I enjoy the game,' he said.

The other tin men, sensing a contest, began crowding round them.

'Why don't we play a little game of eight ball?' said Tilley lightly. 'If I lose, I consent to the divorce . . . if you lose, you give Nora up . . . walk away from her.'

BB stared at Tilley who stared back at him.

'Rack 'em,' BB said quietly.

BB smiled. If this was another of Tilley's setups it was backfiring on him badly. BB had what must surely be a winning break. One by one he was sinking every ball on the table. He lined up the cue ball on a seven ball and it neatly dropped into the pocket. Quickly moving around the table, he lined up another shot and once more sunk the ball.

Tilley was looking worried as BB moved, quickly and confidently, towards victory.

'Combination – side pocket,' BB muttered.

It was a particularly complicated shot and as BB hit the ball and sunk it, several of the tin men could not refrain from clapping – until a glower from Tilley made them shut up.

'That's four,' said BB.

He quickly surveyed the table and saw his next shot. Stroking the pool cue with his fingers he carefully aimed and hit the ball which rolled towards the pocket, but missed it, bouncing back a few inches.

Tilley grinned and went to work, sinking shot after shot as he moved round the table.

Finally there was only the eight ball left on the table. He eyed it for the coup de grace.

'You make this one here, and you win,' said BB, trying to shake Tilley's concentration.

'Don't I know it,' Tilley crowed excitedly, 'don't I know it!'

He took the shot: the eight ball headed for the pocket but didn't make it, hanging up on the felt about two feet from the pocket.

'Bad break,' BB said without much sympathy.

Deftly he moved into action, sinking every one of his balls until he only had the eight ball to sink. He eyed it carefully while Tilley eyed him nervously.

A couple of the tin men were making private side bets.

BB lined up the shot, taking his time. At last he took the shot – and missed. The eight ball lingered on the lip of the pocket.

'Tough break,' Tilley sang, moving in and quickly sinking the eight ball.

'You lose,' he said smugly.

'Yeah,' BB agreed. 'That puts an end to one of our differences. Now, concerning you . . .'

'Yeah?' Tilley challenged him.

'I'm gonna beat the crap out of you,' BB growled.

'You want it here or do you want it outside?'

'Outside,' Tilley replied, narrowing his eyes to two tiny chinks.

BB turned to move towards the door and Tilley, wasting no time, swung with all his might and hit him on the back of the head. As BB began to stagger Tilley got ready to hit him again but BB suddenly whipped round and smashed him in the face, knocking back. He was about to move towards Tilley when the other tin men tried to block him.

'Stay out of this,' Tilley gasped, getting to his feet. 'This is between the two of us.'

The two tin men eyed each other, dodging and weaving. Suddenly, with a remarkable, catlike speed, BB landed four hits to Tilley's stomach and one to his head, so that he fell into the rack of pool cues which crashed to the ground. BB was about to jump on him when he slipped on one of the cues and tumbled over.

Wing, watching the fight at the office door, shook his head with disgust.

Again the two men got to their feet and as Tilley moved towards him, BB again hit Tilley hard in the stomach. Undeterred, Tilley kept coming at BB and finally rammed him, knocking him back on the ground. As he pushed BB's head to the ground, and tried to hit it against the floor, BB managed to get a hand free and hit Tilley hard on the side of the head.

The tin men had seen enough: they jumped in and pulled the two apart.

'That's enough you guys,' Sam grunted, as he dragged BB away from Tilley.

'Come on, break it,' gasped Mouse as he took hold of his new partner.

BB and Tilley stood up, brushing their suits and straightening their ties.

'I think our business is finished,' said BB.

Tilley just stood and watched as BB walked up the steps of the steps of the pool hall and departed.

Chapter Twenty-Nine

'... improves the insulation...' came the familiar chant.

'... we'll have a representative in your area...' went the chorus.

In Superior's back office the tin men had got down to their second main topic of conversation.

'... Danny's an example of that,' Looney was saying. 'Danny goes into a bar, chicks lined up and down the bar. Walks up to one and says, "Honey, would you like to fuck?" She slaps him in the face. He'd move down to the next girl, say the same thing... she'd slap him. Then he'd just keep moving down, going from one girl to the other. Fifteen, maybe sixteen girls would tell him to get lost... to get the hell out of there...'

Unnoticed by the tin men who sat around Looney's desk drinking coffee, BB walked into the office, still looking disheveled and with a bruise on his cheek. He walked over to the coffee machine.

'... call him names,' went on Looney, 'but he doesn't take it personal you see... he keeps going, and then the next girl smiles. She says, "Why don't you buy me a drink?"... he scores. Every time. He goes through a lot of girls, takes a lot of slaps in the face, but he never takes it personally and he always gets what he wants.'

He looked up at BB who had just come over to join them. 'Hey, Beeb,' he said in surprise. 'What happened to you? That broad beat the shit out of you?'

BB smiled, but Looney was seriously worried.

'I think you must enjoy these masochistic relationships. Smashes your car . . . punches you in the face . . .' He turned to Bagel who had just walked out of his office to hand a file to Nick, one of the tin men.

'Bagel, you ought to get a load of this broad Beeb's messing with.'

'Looks a little too romantic for me,' Bagel remarked, disappearing back into his office.

'You know who's no longer married to who?' said Cheese, embarking on the tin men's third main topic of conversation.

'Well, we ought to know,' Carly replied sarcastically. 'There's like a million fucking people living in Baltimore. How many guesses do we get?'

Someone walked into the office carrying an envelope. 'I have a certified letter here for William Babowski.'

'The guy over there,' said Nick, pointing at BB.

While BB was taking delivery of the certified letter and signing for it, the other tin men were trying to guess who was no longer married to who.

'It's not that hard if you think about it,' said Cheese.

'Ruby and Joe,' Looney suggested.

'No,' Cheese replied, 'but they're friends of them.'

'Friends of them . . .' Looney pondered.

'Ed and Ethel?' said Carly.

'Ed and Ethel aren't that friendly with Ruby and Joe,' Cheese pointed out.

'What are you talking about?' said Carly. 'I went to a party, not two weeks ago at Ed and Ethel's, and they invited Ruby and Joe over.'

'It doesn't mean they're friendly because they're invited to a party,' Cheese contradicted him. 'They're friendly, but not that friendly. Couple I'm thinking about were very, very tight with Ruby and Joe.'

Having signed for the letter, BB opened it and pulled out a Summons. He quickly read:

You are summoned to appear before the Home Improvement Commission at 9:30 a.m. on Wednesday, April 6, 1963.

BB smiled and walked over to Bagel and handed him the Summons.

Meanwhile Looney was taking a pragmatic approach to the question of who was no longer married to who.

'Do we have any money bet on this,' he said, 'because otherwise we could be thinking and not gaining anything from this discussion.'

'Frank and Vivien?' Carly had a stab.

Looney looked surprised. 'Frank and Vivien broke up?'

'I don't know,' Carly sighed, 'I'm just making names up for Christ sake.'

'They did break up,' said Cheese, 'but that's not who I was thinking about.'

Looney grinned. 'I'd like to call on Vivien . . . she's one hot broad.'

'Then why don't you call her?' said Carly.

Looney looked rueful. 'I stood her up in high school . . . she's hated me for nearly fifteen years.'

'You stood up Vivien Marshall?' said Cheese in astonishment. 'Are you an idiot! What an idiot!'

'I stood her up for Denise,' Looney explained, his twitching increasing as his spirits fell, 'who happened to have been my wife. So, yes, I was an idiot. If I knew then what I know now . . .'

'Jesus Christ! I think you should take some legal counsel, Double B,' Bagel was saying on the other side of the office.

'Not necessary,' BB said calmly.

'Better to err on the safe side.'

'I'd rather handle it myself,' BB insisted.

Bagel shrugged. 'Want me to find out what they've got

against you? I know a clerk down there. For a price I could get the inside scoop. These guys are fishing right now.'

BB just shook his head.

Bagel stared at him, 'You okay, Double B?'

'Yeah . . . yeah,' BB nodded.

'Because ever since Moe went down you seem a little off your feed to me.'

BB patted his boss on the shoulder. 'Thanks for the concern, Bagel, but I'll be all right.'

He put the Summons into his breast pocket and walked out of the office.

'What was your ex-wife's maiden name?' Carly was asking Looney.

'Essex.' The name seemed to provoke a complete Morse Code of twitching in Looney.

'Denise Essex.' Carly considered the name. 'Did she have a sister named Wilma?'

'Yeah,' Looney replied morosely, going into a spasm of twitching and blinking.

Garly grinned. 'You're kidding me.'

Cheese was getting irritated. 'What does this have to do with the couple who broke up?'

'We'll get to that once we've discussed Wilma,' said Carly. 'They'll still be broken up . . . we'll get to that in a minute.'

Looney was looking at Carly curiously. 'How do you know Wilma?'

Chapter Thirty

Tilley drove into the parking lot of the Pimlico Hotel and headed for a dark corner where several cars were already gathered. He was about to park his car when he recognised Wing in the car next to his, talking to a guy who looked very familiar but for a few moments he couldn't place him.

Then he did, and he was so confused that he just sat there watching them. After a couple of minutes, Wing got out of the car which began to drive out of the lot. Tilley headed after his boss who was walking towards the bar/restaurant.

'Hey, Wing,' he said as he caught up with him. 'Isn't that the putz from the Commission?' He pointed to the car which was just rounding the bend.

Startled, Wing looked at him. Then he sighed. 'Masters? Yeah.'

'What the hell's he doing hanging around here?' Tilley said curiously.

Wing lit a cigarette, inhaled quickly and exhaled slowly. 'He wants information,' he muttered.

'I nailed his ass the other day, Wing,' Tilley boasted. 'Can't lay a finger on me. I was amazing, you should have been there. I was amazing... I was respectful, courteous, but I was slipping and sliding... they couldn't touch me.'

Wing looked sour. 'I got a real problem, Tilley,' he said bluntly. 'Come inside, I'll buy you a drink.'

'You're gonna sell me out to the Commission? Wing, am I hearing this right?'

Sold out by his own boss. He'd thought that now, when the chips were down, when the IRS had his house and Marengay had his wife, his partner had run out on him and the Commission were gunning for his livelihood, that the company he'd given his life and soul to would stand by him. And here he was being sold down the river.

'I'm up front with you about this,' Wing said gravely. 'I'm upfront with ya, Tilley. I've got my balls in a vice . . . what am I gonna do?'

'Is this about the money I owe you?' said Tilley, trying to get a handle on Wing's motivation. If he could do that, then maybe he could strike some kind of deal with him and Wing might even be able to renegotiate with the Commission. It was still possible.

'Are you just pissed?' he went on desperately. 'You want to get even because of the horse race? I told you it was an accident.'

'Tilley, it's got nothing to do with the money,' Wing said wearily.

Tilley stared at him.' You're selling me out? You're gonna let them bury me? Jesus Christ, Wing . . . Jesus Christ! I'm not gonna be able to work in this business? Wing, this was my chosen field!'

Wing tried to make him understand. 'Masters was gonna take this company apart. You're the low man on the totem pole, Tilley. There's a lot of guys earning a good living . . . no sense for it all to go up in smoke. You understand, don't you Tilley? It's just business.'

'Jesus Christ!' He knew what a drowning man must feel like.

'Listen, Tilley,' Wing said magnanimously, 'you owe me sixteen plus from the race and you're in for over two grand on the books, so I tell you what . . . I'll wipe the slate clean.' He took out his wallet and peeled off a few notes. 'Here's a thou until you get yourself set up. I can do no better than that.'

'You'd sell me out for a lousy three thousand dollars?' Tilley stared with disgust at the money. 'Three thousand dollars and I got to go down the toilet? Jesus Christ, Wing, how long the two of us been busting our asses together . . . Jesus Christ! We got some history to this relationship for Christ sake. Masters puts a little squeeze on you, you just sell out. Three thousand dollars!'

Wing was through with explanations and apologies. 'The bottom line is, I'm running a business, Tilley.' He peeled off another couple of hundred dollars from his wallet. 'Here's another deuce.' He looked at Tilley and shook his head. 'I carried you a long time, Tilley. I've done a damn sight more than a lot of guys would have done for you . . . and I don't see no gratitude from you.'

He got up to leave. 'You can finish up whenever you like.' He threw a few dollars on the table for the drinks. 'I'm sorry, Tilley. That's the way of the world.'

He patted Tilley on the back and left the bar.

'Bill!' Nora called up to BB. 'Better hurry up, everything's ready!'

She was serving up breakfast – eggs, bacon and hash browns – when he wandered into the kitchen a few minutes later, tying his tie.

'I can't believe that you're up so early,' she smiled. 'This is a rare occasion.'

'Yeah. I just got some business downtown I gotta take care of.'

He watched her preparing the plates of breakfast, knowing that he'd have to tell her.

'Toast will be ready in a second,' she said, unaware that he was watching her. 'Coffee's on the table.'

'Listen, Nora,' he said hesitantly, as she waited for the

toast to pop up out of the toaster. 'I . . . um . . . I . . . er . . . lied to you the other day.'

'How so?' she said absently, peering into the toaster to see if the toast was getting brown.

'I went to see Tilley about the divorce,' he confessed.

She turned to look at him.

'He was not too agreeable,' BB went on, 'and one thing led to another, and we decided to shoot some pool to settle the matter.'

'What!'

The toast popped up.

Nora ignored it, staring at him, thunderstruck.

BB shrugged. 'We played pool. If I won he'd give you up, if I lost I'd give you up.'

'You played pool for me?' she said tonelessly.

He knew what it must sound like, but what could he say? 'Nora I had no choice.'

She spoke slowly and deliberately. 'It's the most despicable thing I've ever heard in my life. I mean, it's disgusting . . . guys shooting pool to determine my future.'

'Nora, I had no choice!' he repeated. 'Hand me the toast,' he added unthinkingly.

'Get the toast yourself,' she snapped.

'I'm just trying to be honest,' he explained, taking the toast out of the toaster. 'It's been on my mind . . . on my conscience.'

He picked up one of the breakfasts. 'This plate yours or mine?'

'Why don't you take both,' she said angrily. 'Maybe you can choke to death on one of them.'

He took one of the servings and sat down at the table while Nora stared at him, amazed at his inability to recognise the seriousness of the situation.

'How can you be so . . .' she shouted at him, 'how can you not understand how wrong that is? I can't understand that mentality! Shoot pool for me! It's insane.'

BB was busily dipping his toast into his eggs. 'Tilley is not the most rational man in the world,' he said. 'I tried to talk to him . . . he wouldn't listen. So, what are my options? You know what I'm saying? What are my options?'

'I can't believe you had to shoot pool!' she wailed. 'Don't you understand that . . . don't you understand how crazy that is? You're sitting there . . . you're eating your eggs as if it's normal business in life here! Like feudal lords or something you used to read about in history books.'

He held up his hands. 'All right, I'm sorry.'

He ate in silence for a minute until Nora's curiosity got the better of her.

'What happened?' she asked.

'I lost.' He dipped more toast into his eggs.

'You lost?'

'I blew the eight ball,' he explained sadly.

'You lost?' she repeated, still not understanding.

'Yeah.'

'What does that mean?'

'It means I'm supposed to give you up, and I'm never supposed to see you again,' he said, his mouth full of breakfast.

Nora lost patience. 'Will you stop eating the eggs for a minute!' she shouted. 'How can you tell me things like this and casually eat your eggs? What does this mean, Bill?'

'Well,' he considered the question for a few seconds, 'I'm supposed to give you up as part of honoring that agreement, but I'm not that honorable a guy.' He grinned and took a quick sip of his coffee. 'I gotta go.'

Nora put her hands on her hips. 'Why are you running off so fast here?'

'I told you,' he said, getting up to leave and giving her a quick kiss, 'I got some business downtown.'

He was about to leave the kitchen, but stopped at the door, turning back to give her a longer, passionate kiss to which she responded warmly.

'I'll see you later,' he said.

Nora followed him to the front door and stood watching as he got into his baby blue Cadillac and drove away.

Chapter Thirty-One

Tilley felt like a stiff that had been dragged out of the bay. He had, it was true, spent the night in his Cadillac in a vacant parking lot overlooking the harbor. He could see no way forward and no way backward. He had been robbed of everything – except his precious Cadillac and it was on the cards that they'd be helping themselves to that too in the near future.

He pulled his car into a parking space just a little up the street from the tobacco warehouse which housed the Home Improvement Commission and made his way towards it.

He seated himself on a bench against a wall in the corridor off the main Hearing Room, waiting for the session to begin . . .

When BB walked through and sat down on a bench opposite, their eyes met, glanced off each other, dropped to the floor and up to the ceiling, and finally met again.

For once it was Tilley who broke the ice.

'You gotta testify, huh?' he said awkwardly.

BB nodded. 'You?'

'Yeah.'

'You got a lawyer?' BB asked.

'Nah,' Tilley said confidently. 'I already testified once. I beat 'em before, I'll beat 'em again.'

They sat in silence for another minute or so, then Tilley asked casually, 'You got a high-priced mouthpiece to speak for ya?'

BB shook his head. 'I don't need one. I don't expect to win.'

Tilley raised an eyebrow. 'How so?'

'I gave them some pretty incriminating evidence.'

'You gave them evidence?' Tilley said in astonishment.

'The only way I could think to get out of this business.' He smiled.

'Hey, that's good,' Tilley pointed at him, laughing, 'that's good, yeah.'

'The hearing for the Home Improvement Commission is now in session,' came a voice from the hallway.

Tilley got to his feet. 'So . . . how's Nora?' he asked uncomfortably.

'She's doin' all right,' said BB.

'Ernest Tilley?' said an official, coming out of the Hearing Room.

'Yeah . . . here,' he said, then turned back to BB. 'Take good care of her,' he added gruffly.

The Hearing Room seemed to be more crowded than on the previous occasion. Maybe the press had been alerted that there had been some dramatic new developments, because the observers' gallery was now filled with journalists, concerned businessmen from allied trades, and former customers anxious to see justice done and dignity restored.

Masters was once more at the microphone. 'Are you aware that that's a violation of Sections 258 and 261?' he was asking Tilley.

'I'm not aware of the section numbers,' he replied. 'Sometimes you get a little over-zealous in the heat of the sales pitch, that's all.'

Masters' interrogation technique, backed up with some solid evidence, had at last acquired a cutting edge. 'Was it the heat of the sales pitch on February 23rd of this year that made you write across a contract, "This Job Is Free"?'

At the Defense Table, Tilley shifted his feet and found himself sweating. 'As I remember, no sale was made concerning those customers,' he said cautiously.

'It fell out because a loan couldn't be arranged, but the people did agree in principle,' Masters reminded him.

Tilley didn't reply.

'The point that we'd like to stress is that you misled these people,' Masters went on. 'Told them the job was free. Then you sent in your closer with some cover story about how you had suffered a nervous breakdown, and a sale was ultimately made for twenty-three hundred and seventy-seven dollars. That is misleading and deceptive sales practice.'

Tilley began to wriggle. 'It was temporary insanity. I don't know . . . it just came over me . . . it might have been something I ate. I don't know . . . it was crazy, I'm the first to admit it was a crazy thing to do. Believe me —'

Masters cut him off. 'We have other specific examples of deceptive sales practice on your behalf concerning a job carried out on December 11, 1962. You violated Sections 241 and 247. And concerning a job sold to Mr and Mrs DeFranco on October 9, 1962, violations of Sections 251 and 257 took place.'

Tilley was clinging to straws. 'What are all these numbers here?' he asked. 'I'm not familiar with all these section violations.'

Masters ignored him. 'It is the feeling of this Commission,' he declared, 'that these infractions are severe violations of the Home Improvement Laws, and therefore constitute misuse of the license to sell aluminum siding as approved by this State. It is the decision of this Commission to revoke your license to sell aluminum siding which will prohibit you from practicing in the State of Maryland.'

'Are you sure?' Tilley blustered. 'Maybe the guys want to think this over.'

'Thank you, Mr Tilley,' Masters said sternly. 'You may hand over your license to the Clerk of the Commission on your way out.'

Was that it?

For once, there was no slipping and sliding for Tilley. He was all out of tricks.

In a daze he got up from the table and walked to the door. He stopped at a desk where the Clerk was sitting, pulled out his wallet, took out a small document and mechanically threw it on the table. Then he left the building.

'Will Mr William Babowski please come forward,' Masters said into the microphone.

BB walked over to the Defense table and sat down.

'You have the right to have a lawyer present if you so wish,' Masters advised him.

'I do not wish,' BB replied emphatically.

Chapter Thirty-Two

Still unable to think straight, Tilley shambled down the street towards his car – and then suddenly realised that there was an empty space where it should have been. He stared around in confusion, trying to remember where he'd parked it.

A young black kid saw him looking and walked up to him. 'Did you have a car parked here?' said the kid. 'A Cadillac?'

Tilley eyed him suspiciously. 'Yeah. What about it?'

'A man told me to say they took it.'

'Who took it?' He looked up and down the street but there was no one else around.

'Man said, the tax man,' said the kid indifferently. Gave me a dollar to tell you so.'

He wandered off, leaving Tilley standing there in the void where his Cadillac had been.

'Tax man!' he muttered. 'Fucking IRS. How low can you get? How low can you get?'

He walked around in his Cadillac-shaped void as if somehow it might miraculously re-appear.

'They're low life,' he mumbled. 'How can people come and take a man's car . . . His Cadillac?'

'I think with the number of violations on your record, Mr Babowski,' Masters concluded, 'this Commission has no recourse but to revoke your State license.'

Sitting in the observers' gallery, Stanley Franks

listened attentively and with great satisfaction as Masters added, 'Would you please drop off your license with the Clerk of the Commission on your way out.'

BB leaned into the microphone. 'Thank you.'

He walked quickly to the Clerk's desk and tossed the document carelessly on the table before heading out the door.

Walking down the street towards his car he noticed Tilley standing in his vacant parking space.

He stopped.

'Sorry about your license,' he said.

Tilley gazed at him with a stunned, lost look on his face. Then he seemed to remember.

'Yeah,' he sighed. 'You in there?'

'Yeah,' BB nodded. 'They got my license as well.'

'Sorry to hear it.'

The two ex-tin men stood in the street, like low noon.

'What are you doing standing there?' said BB.

'This is where my car used to be,' Tilley said, but there was a question in his voice, like he was not sure that he could even back that statement up.

'Stolen?'

'IRS,' Tilley growled, pouncing on the name like a dog who'd dug up an old, almost forgotten bone.

'Fucking bandits! Bandits! Thieving sons of bitches!' he cursed.

BB stood looking at Tilley for a moment.

'You need a ride home?' he asked.

'I could use one,' Tilley muttered.

'Come on.'

They crossed the street towards BB's baby blue Cadillac.

'Some bullshit Commission, huh?' said Tilley as BB drove through town. He seemed to have perked up a lot and had found, to his surprise, that Marengay wasn't

such a bad guy after all.

'Tell me,' he went on with righteous indignation, 'where's it written in the Constitution that says you can't hustle for money? Where's it written? It ain't like I went into an alley and hit a guy over the head with a brick and stole his money... not like I broke into somebody's house and stole his stuff. All I'm doing is selling... where's the crime in that?'

'I don't know what the world's coming to,' BB agreed.

'You're telling me,' Tilley sighed. 'I don't know what the world's coming to.'

'You know what our big crime is?' said BB. 'We're nickel and dime guys. We're small-time hustlers. They got us because we're hustling nickels and dimes.'

Tilley thought about this. 'Nickels and dimes. You got a good point there, BB. You're right on the money with that kind of thinking.'

BB brought his Cadillac to a halt at a Stop sign and glanced out of the window as a Volkswagen Beetle drove across his path at the crossroads.

'Gotta find a new business to get into,' he said, musing.

Tilley looked dubious. 'New? Very hard to find something new to get into.'

'Maybe,' said BB, stepping on the gas and driving off. 'Maybe not.'

'Better put on my thinking cap,' said Tilley.

'You know,' BB remarked by way of conversation, 'I hear the new Cadillac's gonna be out in a couple of months.'

'You're kidding.'

'Yeah... they're changing the body. I hear it's a beaut.'

'Maybe I should put in my order now,' said Tilley.

'What're you talking about?' said BB, taking his eyes off the road to glance at him sceptically. 'You ain't got a

pot to piss in.'

'Give me the pot,' replied Tilley confidently. 'I'll fill it.'